Also by Courtne Comrie
Rain Rising

RAIN REMEMBERS

Courtne Comrie

HARPER

An Imprint of HarperCollins*Publishers*

Library of Congress Control Number: 2023934253
ISBN 978-0-06-315977-8

Typography by Carla Weise
23 24 25 26 27 LBC 5 4 3 2 1
First Edition

This book is dedicated to
those remembering / trying to
remember to love themselves.

1. FIRST DAY OF HIGH SCHOOL

Two weeks ago
Mom and I traveled with my big brother   our *Xander*
to his university to get him settled into his new
    life.

Two weeks ago
Mom prayed in his dorm room that last year's *incident*
that made national news
    that could've taken his life
                wouldn't follow him and
                    haunt him there.

Two weeks ago
X made me pinky-promise to let him know anytime my
    sadness
became too dark for me to handle.

Two weeks ago
my tears soaked through X's university T-shirt
so much so that his roommate laughed and said,

"I guess she's really *Rain*, huh?"

Two weeks ago
which feels like yesterday
and   forever ago
              at the same time
changed everything up   again.

It's so strange
not racing Xander to the bathroom,
or cracking jokes,
or seeing him check himself in the mirror to make sure
    his hair is lined up
just right.

It's so strange
not watching him cook his famous spaghetti
or dance to the music coming from his speaker,
waving his hands at me and Mom saying,
    "Let me see what y'all got!"

It's so strange
not seeing him, along with
Zachary aka Zach,
Julanie aka Jay,
Andre aka Dre Dre,
or Nicholas aka Butter   *'cause his game's smooth*

eating up all the food and
yelling about some sports team
in our living room.

It's so strange
not hearing him tell me,
         "You've got this, Rain-drop."
or
         "Inhale and exhale."
or
         "Everything's going to be okay. I promise."

It's so strange
not having my
second sunshine who   causes me to rise
         in the morning   from his light.

    "Rain!"
    "Coming, Mommy!"
I walk into the bathroom.
I think I look okay.
I'm wearing jeans and a T-shirt.
I still have in my summer extensions,   knotless braids
    that
Xander had said made me look "real teenager-ish."
I remove my hair scrunchie and let the braids fall to the

middle of my back while looking
at myself in the mirror.
I don't look too long   or else I'll regret *everything*.
I walk into the living room and Mom's got the biggest
     smile on her face
as if she's won the lottery or something.
But I know it's because her little girl   her *Rain*
is—*time has just flown by*—in high school.
     "Guess who's on the phone for you?"
I grab her cell phone and see Xander on her screen.
     "Xander!"
     "Good morning, Rain-drop, ready for your first
          day?"
I look up at Mom, then back at him.
     "I think so."
     "You are, trust me."
I watch him lean back into a stack of pillows.
     "Wait, why are you still in *bed*?"
He laughs,   which warms my heart,
               which makes me miss him even more.
     "My classes start later this afternoon. That's college
          life, sis."
I roll my eyes.
     "Okay, okay, show-off."
I watch his smile fade.
     "Nah, for real, though, Rain, you got this. City High
          isn't anything to be afraid of. Plus, you've been

there before."
I look back up at Mom,   wondering
if she can hear the increased drumming   of my heart.

"Okay," I breathe.

"I'll text you a little later, okay?"

I nod.

"Okay."

"You got this."

I got this.

2. CITY HIGH SCHOOL

When I get off the bus and walk into City High School
I've never seen this many students in my *life*.
I've never seen hallways this crowded   and loud.
I feel my stomach   cramping up   with anxiety.
Breathe, Rain, breathe.
I text the group chat that I'm in with Alyssa and Umi:
It's crazy in here! Wya?

"Ayo, Rain!" Umi.

I spin around and see Alyssa and Umi frantically
      waving me down

from the opposite end   of the hallway.
I try not to bump into anybody as I make my way
     through these waves.

                              This sea of students.

It's so crazy that at City Middle School I felt average
     height   borderline *tall*
and here I feel
tiny.
Almost invisible.

          "Rain!" Alyssa squeezes the life out of me
as if I just returned home from the army,
as if I weren't at her house just a few days ago.
Umi hugs me next, then I
take a step back.
Although I've hung out with Alyssa and Umi all
     summer
they look different
somehow,   *older*
in their faces   and bodies.
In this *new* space   they look
new too.

          "We have some freshman assembly first period."
Umi's deepened voice shakes me out of
my thoughts.

          "I still can't believe our schedules are so different."
          Alyssa.

We all look down at our schedules, which we're holding
  tightly in our hands.

Obviously freshmen.

I sigh.
Although Alyssa and I only have English and math
  together,
the only thing we both share with Umi is lunch.
  "It sucks for real." Umi. "But we got this."
I can hear Xander in his voice.
  "Where's the auditorium again?" I ask,
although I've been here enough times to know—
my brain feels scrambled in this   crowd.
  "This way, let's go." Umi.
Alyssa and I follow him and
as I'm walking, I look
                     to my right
and make eye contact with a guy who   *I think*
is   staring at me.

3. AT THE FRESHMAN ASSEMBLY

I look down and see a text from Xander:
How's it going???

It's going okay, brb.

Aiight
Although we're not best friends anymore, my Nara
    radar is strong,
and I spot her instantly in the crowded auditorium.
She's cozied up next to Dante,   of course,
and right next to them is Amare   and his new girl,
Brenda.
     "Over here." Umi leads us to three open seats.
My heart is beating so hard and
so fast   it
makes me wonder if I should text Xander about it.
When we sit, I daydream
                         that I'm back at City
                           Middle School.
Sitting in English class with Miss Walia,
or in a counseling session with Dr. McCalla,
or in Circle Group.

I miss Circle Group.

I even miss Mr. Jackson   who only ever asked me
    about Xander   but *still*.

                    It was what I knew.

                    It was all I knew.

                    It was my safe space.

Could this place ever be a safe space?

I lean back in my seat.

I can feel the tears form in my eyes. I try
to wipe them   real quick.

    "You okay, Rain?" Alyssa.

I nod, afraid that speaking will erupt this volcano of
    sadness.

    "Good morning, everyone!"

A woman in a blue pantsuit walks onstage, and
    suddenly the auditorium is
silent.

    "I *said* good morning!"

    "Good morning!" everyone screams in return.

Then some laughs   and the additional

    "Wassup?"

    "What's poppin'?"

    "What's good?"

She raises her hands and instant silence.

Wow.

I look around again.

Is this really only the ninth graders?

"Welcome to City High," she begins. "Welcome to a
　　　new chapter in your life. I am Mrs. Bailey, your
　　　new principal."

"Love you, Mrs. Bailey!" someone shouts out.
Everyone laughs.

"Love you too." She shakes her head. "Again,
　　　welcome. I am excited to have all of you
　　　here. The next four years will go by fast, so
　　　it's important to take high school seriously.
　　　Everything you do here matters. Make the most
　　　of it. City High is a place to grow and become
　　　your best selves to prepare you for your futures.
　　　The choice is yours. Take advantage of every
　　　opportunity and stay focused."

This is already　　so different　　from middle school.
My hands are clammy　　　with sweat.

"The bell for first period will ring in about a minute."
　　　Mrs. Bailey continues. "Again, stay focused and
　　　you will be successful. Have a great day!"

That's it?
The bell rings and everyone is　　　jolted
　　　　　　　　　　　　　　　like lightning
　　　　　　　　　　　　　　　out of their seats.

"Rain, let's go!" says Alyssa, who is excited.
Me, who is terrified, wishing
Mom could come get me and take me　　home
or maybe to Mars.

"Coming!"

I try to follow behind, but lose her and Umi in the
crowd.

I look around frantically.

I feel a tap on my shoulder.

"You aiight?" Umi, who looks so calm, so relaxed.

So *Umi*.

I exhale.

"Do I look all right?"

"Nah." He smiles.

I laugh.

"Where's Alyssa?"

"I don't even know. This hallway is a tsunami, for
real. What do you have first?"

I uncrumple my schedule from my pocket.

"Umm . . . gym."

"Gym first period? Damn."

"I know, right?"

"Aiight, so the gym is that way." He points behind
me. "I have science upstairs somewhere. Text me
if you need me, okay?"

I nod.

"Okay."

He walks off.

"See you later, Rain-drop."

I shake my head.

"Later, Umi."

4. I OPEN THE DOOR TO THE GYM

And find a hallway
leading me to *another* door.
I open it and gasp   slightly.   *Locker room.*
Lockers and
benches
and stalls without doors on them.
Nope, not happening.
At City Middle School
we had a very small locker room that no one
ever used.
We just   wore our sweats to school   and
              wore our sweaty clothes for the rest of the day.
I look around and can tell that no one's in

      here   *changing,*   but I can hear a voice
coming behind *another* set of doors.
When I walk through them
the gym seems bigger than I remember it
with the bleachers up.

      "Stand against the wall, everybody!" A man in
athletic gear holding a clipboard.

It's a lot of us who make our way to the side.
Not just girls either   but *boys*,   boys are in here.
Oh God.
I'm trying not to make eye contact with anyone
as I look to find a familiar face,   but I don't.
The gym teacher paces a bit.
> "I'm Coach Fisher, and I'll be your gym teacher this
> year. You show up on time, be dressed in proper
> workout attire, and participate. No cell phones.
> Please know, we do indeed have summer school
> for gym. It is a graduation requirement, so it's
> up to you whether you pass or not."

Summer school for *gym*?
> "Okay, now for attendance." He flips the papers in
> his clipboard.

I can feel the sweat under my armpits.
As he calls names, it confirms I'm in this class without
anyone I know;   therefore
I try not to be noticed.
I'm almost *always* the very last person to be called
during attendance
because my last name starts with a *W*,
which is usually a relief,   but today
feels like impending doom.
> "Rain *Washington*?"

I raise my hand.
> "Here."

He squints at me.　　　My heart stops.

I think of Xander.

I think of the incident.

Does he know him?

"I've never seen you before, Rain. What grade are
　　you in?"

Oh God.

"Ninth."

"Ah, a freshman, that's why. Anyone else here in
　　ninth?"

Not one hand goes up.

If I were a snowman,　I'd melt

immediately.

"Okay, then." He pauses. "Well, today will be open
　　gym. Next time, make sure that you're all
　　dressed and ready to go. We will meet outside
　　on the track."

A mix of cheers and groans.

What's open gym?

I watch as Coach Fisher walks over to a large bag and
　　rolls out several

basketballs.

Some people start grabbing them and teaming up.

Some people start just walking around the gym.

Some people sit in corners of the gym floor.

I guess this is open gym.

I decide to follow the sitting idea.

I take my book bag off my back and hold it in my
        lap   and think back to the days when
the first day of gym included
icebreakers,   sometimes music,
and definitely included everybody I *knew.*
I can tell that I hate gym already but
can't help but watch   with a small smile   one of the
        games
directly in front of me.

                The sound of the basketball against the gym
                        floors
calming my nerves.
I can't help but miss watching Xander   and his best
        friends
play when we were younger.
But now they're in college
while I'm stuck in City High   in this open gym class
as the *only* freshman.

                                My nerves have me
                                sticky with
                                sweat.

Sigh.
        "All right, the period's about over! Let's go! Let's go!"
Everyone's throwing their ball to Coach Fisher
and finding an exit.
There are just so many   exits   that I don't know
        which one to choose.

I follow behind a group of people who also sat on the
    gym floor.
            "Rain." Almost a whisper.
I look up and look back, and it's that guy that
I've seen   *I think*
staring at me   *I think*
in the hallway,   but
he's walking away.
Did he say that?
Did he say my name?
Was he in here the whole time?

5. SUPPLIES AND EXPECTATIONS

Every class is
supplies   and   expectations.
                And me sitting up in front,   so I don't
                    have to look at anyone but
the teacher.

But when the teachers call my name
I see how they do a double take,

a squint,
a tilt of the head.

                              How the name
                                  Washington
                              rings a bell.
                              How I kind of look
                                  like that Xander kid
                              from the news.
It makes me think
about that time when
Mom prayed for Xander in his dorm room. And I
    wonder
if she should've *also* prayed
that last year's *incident*
that made national news
            that could've taken X's life
wouldn't follow *me* and
            haunt *me*   *here*
                              too.

I almost cry when I walk into English class and see
    Alyssa.
    "Rain!" She waves me down to the empty seat next
        to her.
    "Wassup, Rain?"
I look behind me and see Amare.

Finally,   *my people.*

"Hey, Amare."

As students are still walking in,

I turn to Alyssa.

"You seen Umi?"

"Yeah, a couple of times. How has it been so far?"

"It—"

"All right, everybody, settle down, settle down."

The teacher.

And it's not Miss Walia,   not even *close.*

He walks around, handing out papers.

"I am Mr. Allen, and today we'll be going over
the supplies needed for this class and classroom
expectations."

6. ANOTHER THING DIFFERENT

When Alyssa and I walk into the cafeteria,

it's crowded,

it's loud.

I swear the lunch line looks like they're giving away
free sneakers or concert tickets,

rather than the rectangular pizzas and milk that I see
    on people's trays.
    "Wow," Alyssa says. "It's crazy in here."
We start walking slowly
around
            looking for Umi
until I hear,
    "Rain!"
We both spin around to see if it's Umi,   but it's not.
It's Amare at a table with Nara, Dante, and their crew.
And although this was my *old* crew,   well,
more like the crew I was connected to through my *ex-
best friend*, Nara,
I'm grateful for the familiarity.
We walk over and Amare stands up to give us hugs.
    "Hey, guys," I say.
    "Hey!" says Brenda, Amare's new girl.
    "Wassup," says Dante, who sits there all confident,
like he's been in ninth grade before.
    "Hi," Nara says lightly.
She's twirling the braids in her hair, which are like
    mine.
I wonder if she notices.
    "Hey," I say back.
So *awkward*.
    "How y'all liking City High so far?" Dante says.
    "It's . . . ," I begin.

"Different," Nara and I say at the same time.

We look up at each other, then look away.

More *awkwardness.*

I blurt out,

"Amare, are you coming to flag practice this week?"

Dante looks up at me.

"Flag practice? What you mean, *flag* practice?"

Amare's eyes grow large like a ghost walked by.

I guess what I said was worse.

Oops.

I forgot no one knows.

"Nah, nah, I help them clean up after! Rain does
this—flag thing. Like dancing with flags . . .
Uhh, at the church . . . Yeah, my mom got me
helping them set up and stuff . . . Uhh, I guess
she'll force me to help this week again too!"

"Ohhh, okay." Dante now has his phone to his face.

I mouth to Amare,   *Sorry,*   when no one's
looking.

He shakes his head.

"Oh, y'all over here?"

Umi. *Finally.*

He daps everybody up, even people I've never really seen
him talk to before.

I guess he appreciates the familiarity too.

"We were looking for *you.*" Alyssa.

"I found us a spot over there." He points at a table in

the far left corner of the cafeteria.
We wave goodbye to Nara and her crew.

When we finally sit,
in true Alyssa fashion,
she's already giving me and Umi
parts of her lunch to sample.
    "Good, right?" she asks.
We nod and
I've never been so grateful for cold food.
What I discovered this summer was that Alyssa
    absolutely loves to cook.
Her family is close and celebrates often.

With a mouth full of food,
Alyssa says,
    "I heard they don't have a step team here. Like most
        of the team graduated, so they don't have one
        right now."
Another thing   different.   *Great.*
How I miss
the steps,   the music,
that our hands to legs,
our feet to floor,   would make.
I sigh.
    "How were your classes?" I ask Umi.
He shrugs.

"It was aiight, I guess. Nothing special. My teachers
        are okay. Yours?"
I hear him, but all of a sudden,
I'm making eye contact at the table directly across from
        us
with the guy,   *that same guy*
        who was looking at me in the hallway.
                The one *I think*
        I saw at the end of gym class,   who *I think*
        said my name.
But this time
I don't have to think because   right now   he's
        definitely looking at me

                                staring at me
from where he's at.
                        Does he know Xander or something?
He nods his head at me.
My stomach sinks.
What—
        "Rain, you good?" Umi.
I break the stare,   my heart beating faster.
        "Um, yeah, same. Classes are nothing special."

7. A LOUD SILENCE

The last time Mom
and I were alone   together   like this,   *for this
        long,*
was when Xander got hurt.
And sometimes,   not all the time,
I can feel *it*   again.
When I sit on the sofa,
turn the TV on,
open the refrigerator,
brush my teeth,
lie in my bed,
walk past X's bedroom and see that it's empty,   I can
        feel it again.
That time.
When everything fell apart.
But it's different now.
X is not in a hospital,   he's at college, even though
it was a *college* trip where it all happened.
But it's now.
He's safe now . . .   *right?*

I wonder if Mom feels the way I feel:

                              the missing with the
                                worrying.
                              The silence being the icing
                                but

this is no piece of cake.
    "How was your first day?"
I hear her, but
missing Xander is a loud silence.
I'm sitting at the kitchen table,
oiling my scalp   as instructed,   while she cooks.
    "It was pretty good."
I tap the screen of my phone.

I can't just call X anytime I want anymore because
his classes run into the evenings.
As if he hears me or *telepathy runs in our bloodline*,
my phone rings.
I almost fall out of my chair   with a smile that could
    stretch across state lines.
That could stretch all the way to him.
I answer quick.
    "Oh, *excuse me*, Mr. Hollywood, you have time for
        me now?"
He laughs.
    "It ain't like that, Rain, you know that. How was
        your first day?"

I exhale.

I want to tell him.

How I hate facing the new.

But he's also facing the new, and I don't want to weigh
     him down   with my problems.

So instead   I say,

     "Everything's cool."

I get up to take the hair oil back into the bathroom.

     "Yeah, that's *real* detailed."

Huh?

     "Huh?"

     "That's vague, Rain. You know we don't do vague
          around here anymore. Mom there, that why?"

     "Nah, it's . . . City High's all right. I'm not sure what
          to say about it. I got some classes with Alyssa,
          none with Umi, though."

     "Oh, *Umi*, huh?" He smiles.

I roll my eyes.

     "He's my *friend*."

     "Yeah, that's how it usually starts."

     "No, it's not like that!"

My mind flashes back to that guy who was looking at
     me,

                         who nodded at me,

                         who stared me down like I owed him
                              money.

I'm not sure if I should tell X about that—

we've never talked about things like *that* before.
I walk back into the kitchen.

"Where's Ma at? Ayo, Ma!"
Mom dries her hand with a small towel and grabs my
phone.

"Hey, baby!"
She wraps her other arm around me,
and it's the three of us again.

I like it this way better.

8. I AM AWAKE

Earlier than usual.

I keep changing my outfit.
I stare at myself in the bathroom mirror way too long.

I change my hair way too much.
I use a face wash that I haven't touched in months.

I see how long I can suck my stomach in for.
I use some extra strawberry lip gloss.

I take some of those deep breaths that I learned
from Circle Group.

I miss Circle Group so much.

"Rain, it's time to go, or you'll be late!"

"Okay, Mommy!"

When Alyssa walks into English class late, I know
it's because she met the school psychologist.
Today is the first day of counseling for the both of us.
After handing Mr. Allen her pass,
she slides into her desk.
I turn to her and whisper,

"How was he?"

"She's nice," she whispers back.

She's?

"Oh, okay."

"When do you see her?"

"Sixth period."

She nods.

I miss Dr. McCalla so much.

I look down at my appointment pass.

"She's nice," she whispers again.

Although Alyssa told me the school psychologist was
    nice,
my stomach hurts anyway.
I sit in her office   waiting for her,
                                    flinching at voices that I
                                        think are hers.

This office is nothing like Dr. McCalla's.

His office had more color,   and he had an oil diffuser
    that smelled real nice.

Sometimes he'd make me pick the scent.

He also had a table with snacks,   and I don't see any
    snacks,

not even mints.

I remember that Xander also

meets with his counselor today.

And this makes me wonder if I should text him
    or not—   maybe just

wait for him to text me   just in case   he's doing
    college things.

Or maybe I—

    "Rain?"

I jump.

    "Hi."

A tall figure walks in and closes the door.

She sits at her desk,

shuffling through paperwork.

She looks up at me.

    "I'm Dr. Sherif. Welcome to City High School, Rain."

Her face is stern,   round,   with rounded clear
    glasses,

nutmeg skin,

hair slicked back into a ponytail.

"Thank you."

"How are you liking it so far?"

Why do her eyes feel like they're staring into my soul?

"It's going well."

She opens a blue folder and starts reading something.

"I know you've seen Dr. McCalla quite a bit."

I nod.

"I'm pretty caught up on a few things, including
      what happened with your brother last year.
        Xander, correct?"

I nod.

"How has that been in more recent days?"

More recent days?

I shrug.

"It's over now."

She stares at me like I'm going to

burst into tears,

so she can hand out

that Kleenex she has sitting on her desk.

I will *never* talk about the incident.

Never.

"That's good." Her face is still stern.

I exhale,   already

hating it   here.

When I'm finally free from Dr. Sherif's office of
annoying questions from someone who barely even
    knows me,
but thinks she *knows* me,
I head to the bathroom.
The bell hasn't rung yet,
so the halls are
empty and actually peaceful   for once.
I pause at a glass trophy case filled with
trophies and old team photos.
    "There's a lot in there, huh?"
A deep voice close behind me.
I freeze.   I can't recognize the voice.
It's not Umi.
I turn around and it's that guy that I saw in the hall,
        the gym,   the cafeteria.
I open my mouth.
    "I—"
He stretches out his hand.
    "Hi, I'm Tommy. And it's Rain, right?"
I shake his hand   with my sweaty one.
He remembers my name.
    "Um, yeah, I'm Rain. We have gym together, right?"
    "Nah, we don't. Not technically, anyway. I'm cool
        with Coach Fisher, and whenever I have a free
        period, he lets me hang in his classes if I lay low
        enough. Guess I wasn't low enough."

He smiles and his teeth are perfect.
Dimples press into his cheeks.
    "Oh."
    "Yeah, I seen you in there. He said your name. I was
        like, *Wow, that name is so dope.*"
It is?
    "Oh, umm, thank you."
    "Dope name for a dope girl, I guess."
Is he talking about me?
His eyes stare into mine.
Should I say something?
    "I—"
The bell rings.
    "See you later, *Rain.*"
He walks off
and I forget
                where I am,
                who I am,
                what I am.

                                    Tommy.

9. I WEAR SWEATS TO SCHOOL

To avoid the locker room fiasco.
There's no way   I'm changing *out of* or *into*
        anything
in front of a bunch of strangers.

When I finally make it to the outdoor track
I realize
having gym first period is worse than I thought it
        would be.
The ground is wet from the morning dew,
and I'm sleepy still.
Plus, it is *way too early* to be out here sweating.

Coach Fisher has us lined up while he completes
        attendance.

> Everyone is
> yawning.

"Today, we'll be doing the mile run," he says.

> Everyone is
> groaning.

He blows his whistle, and we all start running.
Breathe, Rain, breathe.
I'm in a panic because
I'm not a runner   *at all.*
Even though when I was younger
I tried to be as fast as Xander,   it wasn't a hard race
     to lose.
Xander was *always* much faster than I was.
And X being X,   he'd even let me win sometimes,
basically
crawling his way to the finish line   just for me
          to fake a win.
Typical Xander.

I'm hoping,   praying
no one notices me.
I'm hoping,   praying
Tommy doesn't show up.
     "Pick it up, pick it up!" Coach Fisher calls out.
And I just know he's talking to me,   but I have a
     bad habit of holding my breath
anytime I run or do anything that feels   too
     difficult,

                                        or annoying.
I look to my right and there's this girl   *a girl much
     smaller than me*
who is simply walking.

Not even trying to fake jog like me.

    "It's too early for this, Coach!" she calls out.

    "Tiffany, you've said this every day since ninth
        grade! I thought junior year would change
        things!" Coach Fisher calls back.

She laughs it off and keeps walking.

I turn to her.

    "You're right. It's way too early." I repeat her words.

    "Yes, girl."

I walk with her.

A skinny girl not running.

People will think she knows *how* to run but

chooses not to,   which is more acceptable

than a bigger person *like me*   not running.

Seen as   too big

              too lazy

              too unhealthy.

              Seen as   of-course-*she's*-not-running.

She starts talking about her job at an ice cream shop.

And although I'm not really listening to her,

I'm nodding anyway. Just happy to have someone to
    walk with.

When I look across the track

I see someone moving fast   like

a cheetah,

a stallion   running.

My heart stops.

It's *him.*
It's *Tommy.*
And he's getting closer.
And suddenly
I'm aware of my sweat,
smell, hair, height, weight, fingernails,
everything.
"People are so messy with it," I hear.
Huh?
"Huh?" I quickly look behind us.
"With the ice cream." Tiffany.
Oh yeah.
"Ye-yeah, that's true."
"Exactly! My boss is ridiculous too."
I nod as Tommy runs past us.
He looks back briefly, and I swear
he was looking right at me   again.

Umi, Alyssa, and I are walking home
and the sun is so warm
the sky so blue,

                    unlike this morning.
    "My studio art class is so cool and it's in the
        basement of the school too." Umi. "I asked my
        teacher if y'all could come by to check it out and
        he said it's okay."

"That's cool," I say. "Can't wait to see it."

"How was first-period gym, Rain?" Alyssa laughs.

My first thought: *Tommy.*

"It was chilly and wet." I scrunch my eyebrows. "I do
not recommend."

"I can't believe first-period gym is a thing." Alyssa.

"Same." Umi.

We're in front my house.

"See y'all tomorrow. I'll text you guys."

I hug them both.

When I get inside,

I know Mom is still at work because none of the lights
are on.

There's no smell of food,

perfume,   nothing screaming   *Mom.*

I throw myself on the sofa,   exhausted.

I take my phone out and see a missed FaceTime from
Xander.

I dial him back.

"Hey, X!"

"Hold on."

He walks out of his room and into the bathroom.

"Hiding?" I smile.

"Shush!"

He *is.*

I laugh.

"Okay, okay. So, tell me how counseling went."

"Well," he exhales. "It was different."

"Different how?"

"How do I explain this? Umm . . . we didn't talk. I mean, we spoke, but more like introductions. And then he took some cards out and we were playing Uno."

Uno?

"*Uno?*"

"Yeah, I won the first game. He won the second. Then we scheduled our next meeting."

Really?

"That's weird."

"Most definitely wasn't what I expected. What about you? You met the school psychologist yet?"

"Yeah, and she was *so* annoying. She was asking so many questions, and she just met me!"

"I guess. She's just doing her job, though."

He guesses? Why can't he just agree with me?

"I spoke to Dad."

Dad? Why would he speak to him?

"Oh."

I have nothing to say, so he keeps going.

"He was just asking about . . . Rain, you okay?"

"Yeah . . . what'd he want?"

"Just checking in, asking about school and all that. He said he was calling for you, but you didn't want to speak to him."

"Yeah, so?"

"Easy, Rain. I'm just sayin'."

"Yeah, I know."

Silence.

"So, anything new at City High?"

I pause.

"Not really. I'm about to do this homework,
     though."

"Aiight, so hit me up later, then. Love you, Rain."

"Love you too, Xander."

10. DON'T KNOW HOW TO SAY IT

Usually,   when I think of math,
I think of   dread.
I think of the hours Xander spent
trying to explain   *this* equation   or having me
     memorize   *that* formula.
I think of those *times tables*, which,   *to be honest*,
                    still get a little sticky after the fives.
But sitting in algebra with Ms. Familara isn't so bad.

She's this petite, funny thing and we all get to call her
Ms. Fam.
She repeats things   a lot,
          which I need   a lot.
She walks around and makes sure our notes look good
and *roasts us* if they don't.
      "You write this with your eyes *closed*?" She's holding
          up a kid named Trey's notebook.
We're all cracking up.

I text Xander before she catches me with my phone out.
**My math teacher is super cool. I think I'll do good this
    year.**

Instead of the cafeteria
Umi wants Alyssa and me to meet him in the art studio
during lunch.
I see Tommy on our way there, but
                              I don't think he saw me.
When we walk into the art studio, Umi's right:
it's beautiful.
Paintings   murals   miniature sculptures
    everywhere.
He leads us around as if we're touring a museum.
      "Last year's seniors painted this," he says.
A mural of Kobe Bryant and his daughter
playing basketball on a court of clouds.

"Wow." I touch the dried paint of realistic faces.

Alyssa walks over to a table of artwork.

"What's this? Is this Rain?"

Rain? Like me, Rain?

He walks over to her, and I follow behind.

He lifts a canvas with a sketch of my face.

My. Face.

What?!

"That's *me*?"

"Yeah."

I look away from his gaze.

"Oh, why me? What about Alyssa?"

"I thought I'd start off with you. Then Alyssa. Then
    maybe my pops."

"Oh."

I look over at Alyssa, who is all smiles
while I'm all panic,

          embarrassed.

I look back down at it.   It looks so real.   It looks
    like *me*.

Is this from memory?

I suddenly feel like covering my face,

                self-conscious

                    of my imperfect

                        features.

"It's good, so real." Alyssa.

"Yeah," I say.

He smiles.

    "I'm trying. . . . Let's sit over here."

He clears a table of brushes, and we sit as

Alyssa unpacks her lunch.

    "I love it in here." Umi.

Even though I'm freaked out by the sketch, I can

    see why.

It is beautiful.

    "Y'all are still coming to my cousin's birthday party

        tomorrow, right?" Alyssa.

    "Of course," Umi and I say at the same time.

When I get home,

Mom's on the phone.

She mouths, *Dad*, to me.

I nod.

She no longer hands me the phone

like she used to when Dad calls.

She doesn't even look my way   because she knows

    my answer.

Instead

she tells him,

    "She's not ready."

I walk into my room and take out my phone.

I notice X hasn't texted me back yet, and it's been

    hours.

I don't text him again.
He's supposed to text *me* back.

After dinner,
I sit at the kitchen table to finish my homework.
    "Rain!"
    "Coming, Mommy!"
I go into X's room.
Mom's been sleeping in his room   instead of on the
    living room sofa lately.
Which is better for her back.
She hands me the phone.
It's Xander.
                "The workload is *real*, Rain. I'm sorry for not
                    hitting you back."
I'm silent.
I'm hurt, but don't know how to say it.
    "It's okay."

11. A DIALECT I DON'T UNDERSTAND

Umi's dad is the one bringing us to Alyssa's house
for her little cousin's birthday party.

"You look nice," Mom says,
although I'm just wearing jeans and a T-shirt.
    "Thank you," I say,
although   I wonder if she's just saying it
    because I'm her *daughter*,
or because of everything that happened   *last year.*

She styles my braids into one big bun on top of my
        head.
She gives me a thumbs-up.
Her eyes are red, tired, although she's
    dressed for work.
A car honks its horn. *Umi's dad.*
I lace up my sneakers.
    "Have fun, my darling." Mom squeezes me.
I squeeze back.
    "I will, bye, love you!"
    "Love you too!"

When I get into the car,
I say hi to both Umi and his dad,
but Umi only nods my way because he's on the phone.
He's speaking a dialect I don't understand, so I
    know   for a *fact*
that he's speaking to his mom, who's living
in their home country.
He's speaking low,   slow,   and   soft.   I can barely

hear him now.

Is that on purpose?

After his dad lost *his* mom,

Umi's mom went back to their home country when *her*
    mom got sick.

She wanted to be the one to take care of her.

Umi says she's been there for almost three years.

I can remember her slightly from elementary school,
    but not a lot.

Umi usually looks sad when he's on the phone with her,
    although   he won't talk about her much.

The loss of his grandmother and *then* the loss of his
    mom—

a different kind of loss—   but *still*   a loss.

He has a distant mom,   I have a distant dad,

but at least his mom has a real reason to be distant.

Unlike my father who stays away, like suffering from
    an allergy

to family.

I look out the car window to see some of the green
    leaves

spotted orangey brown.

His dad pulls up to Alyssa's house.

    "We're here now, Mom, I have to go." Umi. "Bye, love
        you too."

There's a crack in his voice at the   *love you too.*

His dad looks at us through the rearview mirror.

"You okay, Umi?" he asks.

"I'm solid, thanks, Pops." He opens his door,
       hops out,
opens my door.

"Thank you," I say.
His dad nods.

"Anytime."
But it feels more like a   *make sure Umi's okay.*
I nod back an *I will*   and hop out.

12. WHEN WE WALK INTO ALYSSA'S HOUSE

There're balloons and streamers
of all colors   everywhere,
loud festive music,   cousins running,
laughter, strong smells of food.

"Come, come, come!" It's Alyssa's mom
ushering Umi and me to the kitchen.
Here we go.

I'm already laughing,
                    I'm already excited.
I look over at Umi, who looks the same way that I feel.
Alyssa's home is two stories, and it's her
    family,
her uncle's family,   and her aunt's family, so
    technically *three* families.
Unlike my home, which is mostly quiet,
    Alyssa's house is   always jumping,
                                         always moving,
                                         always celebrating.

Her mom puts trays of food in our hands to bring to
    the backyard.
Alyssa is already out there hanging up more
    decorations.
    "I wonder what the theme is," I whisper to Umi.
    "Everything," he whispers back.
And we both laugh.
And it feels good.
    "Hey, guys!" Alyssa runs up to us, and we're group
        hugging.
We put the food on the table, which barely has room for
    anything else.
    "Sit, sit, sit!" Alyssa instructs,   the way her mother
        does.
And we sit on chairs as more people

and more food arrive.

    "So glad you both could make it!" It's Alyssa's uncle
        Ricky,
who is the father of the birthday girl, Melody, who
        turns ten today.
    "Of course, Uncle Ricky!" Umi stands and hugs him.
I shake his hand.
Uncle Ricky is really nice and cracks some of the
        funniest jokes I've ever heard.
He's always cooking,   always trying to get
        somebody to eat,   *like Alyssa*,
always making sure the people around him are happy.
He's my favorite uncle, Alyssa always says.
I sit back with my eyes closed,
the sun feeling good on my skin.
I wish Mom could enjoy more moments like this,
        instead of working.
I wish Xander could be here with us, instead of away at
        school.
    "Happy birthday to you . . ."
They sing in one language,   then another.
We're all clapping and cheering   as they bring
    Melody out and she's wearing
a big, beautiful baby blue dress—
                  everything's glittering,
                  everything's sparkling,
                  as if her outfit

was made with
the sun's
approval in
mind.
And the cake is *also* blue   and layered   with
    sprinkles   and mermaid tails.
And Uncle Ricky walks her to the middle of the yard,
and they're dancing,
and slower songs start playing.
Something about

                    you're the best thing that
                        ever happened to me.

God blessed me with you.

                    You're so beautiful to me.

Where would I be without you?

                    You mean the world to me.
A lump forms in my throat so heavy,
and tears in my eyes so full,
because all of a sudden,   I'm ten,
with my arms out and no one to dance with.

13. SEASONS

Mom sits with her arm wrapped around me at
    Hope Church
as Pastor speaks on seasons, different seasons,
    new seasons.
    "What season are *you* in?" he asks.
And people clap,
they laugh,   they scream, they dance,   they cry,
    they sing.
I guess the reaction depends on which season you're in.
I wonder what season I'm in.
    High school.
            Xander leaving.
I look at Mom, who wipes a tear from her eye   but
    smiles at me.
Is she happy?   *Is she sad?*
She holds me tighter.
Maybe she's both.
Maybe I'm both.

I have flag rehearsal after church, so Mom is getting a
    ride home from
Amare's mom, Mrs. Porter.

"Hi, Mrs. Porter." She gives me the biggest hug.
"Sweet Rain!"
Didn't I just see her last week?
I laugh.

"You're getting so big!" she exclaims.
I scrunch my eyebrows at Mom.
Big how?
Mom's next with a hug and her gentle

"Have a great practice, darling."
They leave, and I'm walking around the crowded
    sanctuary
looking for Amare like a headless chicken.
I go to the practice room downstairs, and he's already
    there,   unraveling flags.

"What did you do—run down here?"
He looks up at me.

"Sade's not here today, so I thought a head start on
        getting the flags out for everybody would be
        better."
I nod, picking up a flag.
He's right.

"Is she okay?"
Sade is the head of the creative arts here,   including
    flag dance.

"Yeah, yeah. She had to take her mom to the airport." He hands me another flag. "This one is new."

I unravel it, and it's a soft hue of pink with silver trimmings.

"Pretty." I spin with it.

Amare stops and looks at me.

I stop spinning.

"What?"

"You tried to air me out, huh?"

Huh?

"What—"

"In front of Dante and them that time. About me flagging . . ."

I think back.

Oh yeah.

Oops.

"Amare, I am so, so sor—"

"It's cool, I cleaned it up real quick."

I laugh.

"Yeah, I seen that." I pause. "Why don't you tell them? You're so good at it."

"You ever had parts of you that you're afraid to let others know about, for whatever reason?"

My mind flashes back to last year,

before Alyssa and Umi,

before Circle Group,

when I hid behind all that   sadness.

    "Yeah, I have." I twirl the flag in my hand, thinking
of Xander. Of *Tommy*. Of Dr. Sherif.

    "I do."

14. I DON'T SEE

Tommy at gym, but

                  I'm not really looking for
                      him, anyway.

                  Maybe he's absent?

15. INTRUSIVE THOUGHTS

"I know you've struggled with intrusive thoughts."
Dr. Sherif taps her pen against a folder.   I guess *my* folder.

"Used to," I say.

"*Used* to?" She raises her eyebrows.

"Yeah."

"So, no more intrusive thoughts."

Isn't that what I just said?

I exhale.

"I don't think so."

"You don't *think*?"

"I used to have these dark thoughts in my head. I don't get them anymore."

"*Ever?*"

Oh my God.

"Not lately."

"Okay." She leans backs in her seat. "So, what are your *lately* thoughts?"

Uh—

I try to think of my thoughts.

"I don't really have a lot of thoughts."

"No thoughts?"

"I—"

"Give me an example of a thought."

What?

"I don't know. Like, regular thoughts. People have
thoughts, right?"

"So you went from nonstop intrusive thoughts to
now—nothing?"

"Umm, I—I guess. Yes."

"Okay."

"Okay."

Dr. Sherif isn't a Dr. McCalla

or a Miss Walia.

I don't want to pour

myself   out

like barrels,   empty

for her.

16. A TEXT FROM XANDER

My phone vibrates in Global History class.
I look down and see it's a text from Xander:
**Have a good day, sis. Been a busy bee lately, I see. So
have I. Call you tonight.**

17. XANDER DOESN'T CALL ME

Instead
he texts me   a meme
that I don't find that funny.

18. NOW THEY'RE NICE

Mom doesn't wear much makeup,
but while I'm brushing my teeth
I see one of her lipsticks,   *a deep burgundy*,   and
    put it in my book bag.

When I get to school
the first thing I do   is go to the bathroom   and
    apply it to my lips.

                                        My very *full* lips.
It's not as easy as it looks.
It gets all over my hands and
stains my palms like crushed berries,   paint,
                                        or worse, *blood*.
I'm rubbing off the excess from under my nose,   from
    off of my chin.
But I like it.

Alyssa says,
    "*Okay*, Rain, I see you!"

Umi says,
    "That's different." Squints at me. "But it fits you."

When I ask to use the bathroom,   *which I'm doing a*
    lot today,
I walk through all of the halls,   looking around,
    swinging the pass,
rubbing my lips together.

I raise my hand in math class.
    "Ms. Fam, may I use the bathroom?" In my sweetest
        voice.
Alyssa leans over and whispers,
    "Didn't you use the bathroom in English?"
I shrug as if saying,   *I don't know why I keep having to*
    go either.
Ms. Fam points to the hall pass next to the door.
I grab it and
I walk through all of the halls,   looking around,
    swinging the pass,
rubbing my lips together.
    "Rain?"
I freeze.
My heart beats faster.
I know that voice.

I turn around.

"Hi." I give a small wave.

It's *Tommy,* and he's walking up to me. *To me.*

"It's me, Tommy—you remember me, right?"

How wouldn't I?

I stare at his smile again.

Smooth skin, warm eyes, fly outfit.

"Oh *yeah*—from gym class."

He laughs.

"Yeah, I haven't been there for a minute. Been busy
    with homework *already.* These teachers don't
    ever ease up."

"You're right about that."

We laugh *together.*

"You seem pretty cool. I mean, I guess with a name
    like Rain, you gotta be."

"Not as cool as you. I like your sneakers."

He looks down at them and shrugs.

"They're aiight, I guess."

Now he's looking at me so hard   that   I'm not sure
    if he's blinking.

Am I blinking?

I look down at my hands.

"Well—"

"Yo, take my number real quick."

I almost drop the pass out of my hand.

"Your *number*?"

"Yeah, why not?"

I fish for my phone out of my pocket.

As soon as I unlock it,　　　he takes it out of my hand,
　　his fingers touching mine.

He hands it back to me.

　　"Aiight, you got me. See you later, Rain." He gives
　　　me a hug,

and I'm so shocked that I can't even lift my arm.

　　"Later," I try to say as casually as I can as he walks
　　　off.

As he's walking,

he stops　　　and turns back around to me.

　　"Oh, and nice lips, by the way."

　　"Oh—uh—thank—thank you."

He smiles,　　　shaking his head, and
starts walking again.

Oh my God. Oh my God. Oh my God.

Did he just—

And—

What?!

When I get back to math class,

I'm not sure what Ms. Fam is talking about.

My head is spinning　　　in a good way.

I unlock my phone　　and stare at his name, his

number,
that *I* have.

> *The cutest boy I've ever seen.*

I open my camera and stare at my lips like I've never
　　　seen them before.
I used to hate their fullness,
their largeness,　　　　　　　　but now they're *nice.*
Tommy said they're nice.
Tommy said I'm cool.
Tommy likes my name.
Tommy said to take his number.
He said, You got me.
He gave me a hug.

I can still feel his arms,　　　　　still smell his scent.

> *Tommy.*

19. WHEN I GET HOME

I see a missed FaceTime from Xander.
I call him back. He says,
> "Oh, so you're ghosting me now? I called you
> yesterday too."

I sit on the sofa.
> "I'm not. Why didn't you just call me back?"

> "I did, I think. Is Ma home?"

> "No, she's working." I notice the sky behind him.
> > "Where are you going?"

> "To the dining hall. I'm *starved*."

I look over at the kitchen.
> "Me too."

> "Ma cooked?"

> "Nah, but there's leftovers."

> "Wait—Rain—are you wearing *lipstick*?"

My eyes widen. I forgot to wipe it off before I got home.
> "Uhh—yeah."

> "For who—Umi?"

> *"Xander Washington . . ."*

He laughs.

"Uh-oh, the whole name. Okay, I'll stop."

I put the phone closer to my face to see his campus clearer.

"What are you going to eat?"

Background noise.

"X?"

"Yo, Rain-drop, let me hit you back up later. It's crazy loud in here right now!"

"Okay, I'll—"

The phone disconnects.

20. I TAKE A SELFIE WITH MY LIPSTICK STILL ON

One with a filter.

One without a filter.

I like both.

21. WONDERING

The next day in
                history class
                        I'm wondering,

Should I text him?
If not, how will he get my number?
Should I wait?

22. WONDERING, AGAIN

In math class I'm wondering   again.
Should I text now or
           after school?

            Tomorrow?

23. I TEXT HIM

In English class,
I do it,   I text him:
Hi, Tommy, this is Rain! Nice seeing you again!

Was that good?
Was it too much?
                    My heart is racing.

                              I don't hear from him.
                              I don't even see him for
                                    the next few days.
                              No text back, nothing.
                                    Did he get it?

24. HE TEXTS BACK

When I'm walking out of gym class:
3 p.m. tomorrow by the gym

I look around me,   hoping
he doesn't see me all sweaty.

> But I don't see him
> anywhere.

I want to tell him,
*I walk home with my friends, and I don't like walking home
  without them.*
But I don't want to sound like a baby,
and I don't want to *not* see him
and I don't want him to *not* text me back.

So I text back:
Okay.
Was that enough?

I text again:
See you there!

Although
I'm unsure *what* I'm seeing him for.

I'm *hype*,   and I
can't stop smiling.

25. SOMETHING ABOUT YOU

Today Umi and I brave the cafeteria line,
which looks more like an amusement park line.
What probably could've taken five minutes   takes
    almost twenty-five minutes
of standing,   and the occasional clearing of the throat
    when

somebody tries to
cut in front of
us.
Which is then followed by a   *My bad*   and Umi
    saying,   *Yeah, it is your bad,*

which makes me giggle every
                              time.

We both play it safe and get prewrapped turkey
    sandwiches and orange juice.
According to some kids ahead of us, the pizza looked
    sus.

When we get to   what's become   our usual
    table,
Alyssa is already there eating.
    "Oh, you guys survived that line, huh?" Her mouth
        is stuffed
and her face crumbed.
    "Yeah." I exhale as we sit.
I take a bite of my sandwich and as I'm looking up,
I see *Tommy*.
He looks at me,   but looks away.
Maybe he didn't look at me.
Maybe he was looking at someone else.
My phone vibrates.
I look down.   It's *him*,   it's *Tommy*:
Don't forget, 3 p.m.
But when I look back up,   he's *still* not looking at me.
He's laughing with people
who I assume   are his friends.

"You good, Rain?" Umi.

I break my stare.

"Yeah— Um . . ." I pause. "Dr. Sherif is dragging it."

"What happened?" Umi. "I met with her today.

What'd she say to you?"

"She wants to see me after school or something.

Something about *intrusive thoughts*."

I take a sip of my juice.

"Oh, word?" Umi.

"So you're not walking home with us?" Alyssa.

"I don't think so."

"Or do you want us to wait for you?" Umi.

I unlock my phone and text Tommy back,
I didn't forget.

"Nah, y'all can go ahead without me."

After the last period of classes,
Alyssa hugs me.

"You sure you're good? We can always wait for you."

I shake my head.

"I'm sure. You guys go. I'll text the chat when I get
home."

It's only two thirty, so I go into the bathroom
to wait out the thirty minutes.

I look at myself in the mirror.   Fix my hair.
    My shirt.
Look at myself from the front.   From the back.
Okay.
    I think I look okay.

                        I mean, he knows how I look, right?

It's 2:50,   and I don't want to look *thirsty,*
but I also don't want to look like I don't care.
So I head to the gym,
                where he—   *Tommy*—   wants to meet
                    me.
I look and see him—   *Tommy*—
leaned up against a locker,
waiting,
    waiting   for me—   *Rain.*

        My mouth is suddenly dry.

    "Hey, Rain!" He waves.
I like how he says   *Rain.*
I walk up to him,
and he hugs me   again.
I like how he hugs me.
    "Hey." I try not to smile too hard.
He smiles.

"You look cute."

Cute? Me?

"Uh—thank you. So do you."

"Why do you do that?"

Huh?

"Do what?"

"Throw away the compliment."

"I did?"

He squints at me   with a smirk.

I notice how broad his shoulders are.

> How big his hands
> are.

"Yeah, you did." He comes closer to me. "I said you
   look cute. You said *I* look cute. You can just say
   thank you. Actually, you can say, *I know.*"

I laugh   nervously.

"Isn't that rude?"

"Nah. Try it. Here, I'll say it again." He pauses. "You
   look cute, Rain."

"I . . . *know?*"

"Not quite. Give some attitude or something. You
   look cute, Rain."

I laugh.

"I know. *And?*"

He claps.

"There you go!"

He pushes a braid away from my face.

Did I just stop breathing?

"How are you liking City High, by the way?"

His gentle eyes and smile make me look away.

"It's not as bad as I thought."

"Yeah?"

"Yeah."

"If you ever need help with anything, I got you. I
like to give back."

"That's really nice of you. We need more people like
you."

"Ain't that the truth? I saw you, I was like, *Yup, I'm
going to help this beautiful girl.*"

Beautiful girl.

I look away.

"I see you blushing."

I laugh nervously   again.

"So, what's up with you?" he asks.

What?

"What's—"

I look over my shoulder and see Dante leaving through
the main entrance.

Was Nara with him?

"You talking to anybody?"

I look back at Tommy.

"Talking?"

"Yeah, like dating?"

Dating?

"Uh, no . . . no."

"So, we could, like, hang out?"

"Uhh, yeah, okay."

"I don't know, there's something about you. I like
   your vibe. Maybe the mall or something?"

"Uh—yeah, okay."

My stomach is in knots.

Hang out   with a boy,   a sophomore boy,

                                        by myself?

26. I TEXT ALYSSA AND UMI

I'm home now!!

                              How was it with Dr. Sherif?

                                                      Umi.

I don't want to lie.

I'm beat.

27. I FACETIME XANDER

And there's no answer.
I toss my phone onto my bed.

I open my notebooks,
textbooks,
and start working on my homework.

My phone starts vibrating: Xander.
I answer,   half looking into the screen
                half looking at my homework.
   "Rain-drop!"
He's smiling so hard.
   "Hey," I say softly.
   "Wassup, Rain, you good?"
Would you even care if I wasn't?
   "I'm good. How's it going over there?"
   "Aww, that's your *little sister*?" I hear.
I look at my phone and
see a girl standing behind him   looking into his
   phone,

looking straight at me.

Who the heck is that?

"Who's—"

"Rain, call me back in ten minutes?"

I exhale.

"Aiight."

And when I don't,

he does,

but I don't answer.

28. WHILE I'M PUTTING ON MY SNEAKERS

Mom says,

"Rain, I'm making breakfast."

Although I feel hungry,   I remember how tight my

jeans felt this morning.

"I'll get something at school."

She walks over to me and hugs me,

hushed words spoken,

a prayer for protection, I'm sure.

"Have a good day, baby."

While Alyssa and I are packing away books into our
    lockers,
I feel a tap on my shoulder.
Tommy?
I turn around, and it's Umi.

"You scared me," I say,   almost whisper.

"I'm almost done with the drawing."
The drawing?
I scrunch my eyebrows.
He keeps going.

"The drawing of you?"
Oh.

"Oh yeah. That's cool."
I see Tommy and his friends walking down the hall.
Maybe this can be a moment for him to meet Alyssa
    and Umi.
I wave at him.
He looks at me. But keeps walking.

No wave. Nothing.

29. I DON'T BUDGE

I ask Mr. Allen,   my English teacher,
if I can go to the bathroom.
When I walk into the bathroom,   I see
Nara   washing her hands.
     "Hey," I say.
She turns her head to look at me.
     "Hey."
It's always so *awkward* seeing Nara,   even though a
     year ago
she had been my best friend   for basically my
     whole life.
I walk into the stall
and hear that the water's still running.
Why is she still in here?
I finish and flush the toilet
and hear that the water's still running.
That's weird.
I walk out of the stall, and there she is,
     still washing her hands.
I turn on the sink two sinks down from hers

and start washing *my* hands now.

    "I seen you," she says. "After school.

        The other day."

I lose my breath but get it back.

I can see her looking at me through the mirror.

    "Oh, you did?"

I think of that time   after school

when I saw Dante leaving.

I guess Nara *was* with him.

                      Of course.

    "Yeah, you were with that guy—they call him

        something—"

I open my mouth,   then close it.

She squints her eyes, then

opens them wide.

    "T? *Tommy?*"

    "*Oh yeah.* Yeah, I was. He's . . . he's cool. We're cool."

She gives me a look that says,

When have you ever been cool with a guy like Tommy?

but instead she says,

    "Just be careful with him,"

then walks out.

30. I TEXT THE GROUP CHAT WITH ALYSSA AND UMI

Mall on Saturday?
I gotta do something for my pops (Mom related). Umi.
We can wait. Alyssa.
Nah, y'all go ahead. Umi.

31. DIFFERENT

It's Saturday,
and I'm getting ready to meet up with Alyssa at the
 mall.
It feels as if I've been wearing the *same thing*
 the *same jeans*
 the *same shirts*

every day.

When I tell Mom about it,

she says,

"*I* wanted to take you to the mall one of these days,"
     in the most gentle voice.

Mom is not a big fan of shopping,

so I know she would go   just for me.

For me to feel *better*.

For us to *bond*.

She's sitting on the sofa with
     a stack of bills in her lap,

the Holy Bible,   and a smile.

I slide onto the sofa and sit close to her,
     lean my head on her shoulder.

She's so warm.

I wonder why it's been so long since I've done this.

     "Oh, I can—"

     "No, no. You should go with Alyssa. She probably
          has much better fashion sense than I do
          anyway." She laughs. "I guess I can get dinner
          started early. How's her family?"

     "You sure? And they're good."

     "I'm sure." She smiles her tired smile. "Let me go get
          some cash for you."

And when she goes to get money for me,

I feel bad,   I feel guilty,

taking the money   she works so hard for.

> *It's not like we*
> *got it like that*
> *anyways.*

When she comes back,
she holds the money tight in my palm and says,
    "And don't you worry about spending this."

It feels as if Alyssa and I have been in every
    single   store   in this mall.
The bottoms of my feet hurt,   but I haven't found
    anything I like.
We walk into a new store and the first thing I see are
    these blue-and-gray
 cropped sweaters.
I lift one up and hold it against my body.
    "Does this make me look young?"
Alyssa spins around from looking at a table of jeans.
She laughs.
    "Rain, you *are* young. Looks a little short, though."
    "Short because I'm not skinny and shouldn't be
        wearing stuff like this?" I blurt out.
She looks at me,   confused.
    "Not like *that*." She pauses. "I mean, like, would
        your *mom* let you wear that?"
I shrug.

"I don't know."

When I get home,
the first thing I do is hide the bag with the cropped
    sweater
under my bed.
When Mom gets out the bathroom and
         stands at the entrance of my room door,
 she asks,
    "What'd you get?" with the biggest smile.
My heart beats a little faster.
I show her a few shirts and a sweater—   *not* the
cropped one.
    "Me and Alyssa basically got the same things," I say.
    "I like them." She walks over and sits on the bed.
        "How's school, by the way? You barely talk about
        it."
Uhh . . .
    "Well, uhh, it's better than I thought. Like the
        classes are all right. And I'm actually liking
        math with this new teacher."
    "Wow, I've never heard you say *that* before. And the
        new psychologist. What's her name? Dr. . . ."
    "Sherif. Dr. Sherif. She's cool too, I guess. Just
        different."
She wraps her arm around my shoulder and
kisses my forehead.

"Different can be good, if you let it be."

Instantly I think of Tommy.

32. THINKING OF ME

When I wake up the next morning
I see a text from *Tommy*   that he sent me   at
   two in the morning:
Mall next Sunday?
Two in the morning?
He was thinking about . . . me?

             At two in the . . . morning?

I feel warm.
I feel sun.
I feel blue skies.
I feel flowers.

                  I text back:
                     Sure!

I keep my phone in my hand all day
to see if he'll respond.

             But he doesn't.

33. I DON'T WANT TO LIE AGAIN

Sade asks Amare and me to put the flags away after
practice.

"Sade told me you're not coming to flag practice
next week?" Amare.

"Nah, I got . . ."

"What you got?"

He squints at me with suspicion.

"Take it easy, detective. I'm just going to the mall."

"With Umi and Alyssa? You guys are like the three
musketeers."

I just smile.

I don't reply because I don't want to lie   *again.*

34. THE INCIDENT

When Mrs. Porter drops me home   after flag rehearsal,
I lie in bed   trying to think
about what it would be like to be at the mall with
     Tommy.
Walkingtalkingsmilinglaughingholdinghands.
My phone rings.
And although he's never called me before,   I feel in my
     heart that
it's him, it's him, it has to be him!
I take it up and instead of Tommy   it's Xander.
I answer.
     "Hey, X."
     "Rain-drop! *Wah gwan?*" he says in a fake Jamaican
          accent.
It makes me smile, though.
     "What is *wrong* with you? I'm okay, how's it going?"
     "I mean, I haven't been hearing from you a lot lately,
          sis."
I roll my eyes.

Why does he always say that?
He's the one that's hard to reach   not *me.*

I exhale.
I don't say anything.
   "So." He starts again. "I had therapy again
      yesterday."
   "How was it? Y'all still playing Uno?"
He laughs lightly, which softens my heart, so
I laugh with him.
   "Not *exactly.* But we did toss around a football."
Wait—what?
   "A *football?* Wait. I don't—he knows you play?"
   "Yeah, I mentioned it. I mean, he could also look me
      up and find out if he wanted to."
Although he's most likely talking about looking him up
         as in   old football games,
my mind flashes back to the time of the *incident*, when
X was all over the news.
A slight pain hits my chest.
   "Where did this all happen, anyway?"
   "Well, there's this super-long hallway outside of his
      office, so we did it there. Tossed the ball back
      and forth while we talked about some things.
      It was cool. He's a cool dude. His arm ain't too
      rusty either."
   "Wow."

"And how's therapy been going with you?"

I shrug as if he can see it.

"She's still annoying."

He laughs.

"I'm not even touching on that one. But, Rain, it
was good catching up. I'm heading out with
some folks. Call me later?"

No, you call me.

"Okay."

"Okay. Love you, Rain-drop."

"Love you too."

35. THERE'S A TEXT

When I walk into City High

I hear,

"Rain!"

Umi.

He walks up to me and gives me a hug.

I hear a phone alert.

"That you?" I ask.

He takes out his phone to check.

"Nah."

It has to be Xander   or maybe Alyssa   texting me.

I take my phone out and there's a text   from
    Tommy:

Good morning, beautiful.

My pulse increases;   my eyes widen.

I could
        explode.

    "What happened?" Umi.

I stuff my phone into my pocket.

    "Uh, nothing, nothing. Just remembering I, uh, got
        gym first period."

He shakes his head.

    "Tragic."

    "Tell me about it."

36. I TRY NOT TO WATCH

Today
Coach Fisher has us in the gym   playing volleyball.
But this doesn't feel like   *playing*.
Playing is *fun*.   This is working.

We are *working* volleyball.
It's not the big, bouncy, colorful beach ball we used to
    play with in middle school.

> *Of course not.*

It's the small white one.   The *hard* one.
The one that hurts when you get hit with it.
I try to avoid hitting the ball at all costs   and allow
    the more *excited* participants
to do their thing.

> In the middle of the game
> *Tommy walks into the gym.*

I straighten up   interlock my hands
    thumbs on top
knees bent   lean forward   focus on
    the game
as if I were actually   serious about it   the
    whole time.
I try not to watch him   but   I
watch him
walk around   laughing
greeting people like a mayor elect.

> *He's pretty popular.*

Almost everybody in here knows him.

> X would say, *Everybody and their mommas*
> *probably know him.*

I laugh to myself.

When he walks by   where I'm standing
he looks at me   but then looks away   dapping up
        the people around him.
Then he goes and sits on the bleachers
laughing,
laughing, still

                                                without me.

37. AFTER GYM

I hear,
        "Rain!"
But it's not yelled,   it's more sung,
        in two syllables like
                Ra-ain.
I look behind me and see Tommy standing in a corner
        of the hallway
by himself.
He frantically waves me over.
I walk up to him, kind of confused, kind of sad.
        "Hey, I saw you in gym class. I tried to say hi to you."

"You were in there? I didn't even see you!"

He didn't?

I scrunch my eyebrows.

"I was staring right *at* you."

"Really? How could I possibly miss a cutie like
  yourself?"

He smiles,   which makes me smile.

"Hey, listen," he says. "You're still down for meeting
  me at the mall this weekend, right?"

I swallow.

"Yeah, sure, of course."

"Aiight, I'll see you then, pretty girl."

He winks and walks off.

Pretty girl.

      Me,   the

               pretty girl.

38. WHEN I'M WALKING HOME

With Umi and Alyssa
we talk about our day:

the good,

the bad,

the ugly.

Alyssa says,

> "Today was decent. I like the book we're reading
> in English class. My history class is *so* boring,
> though."

Umi says,

> "I'm not really messing with any of my teachers
> except Mr. Travis, of course, the art teacher. The
> workload isn't crazy, though."

I say,

> "I'm still kind of shocked that I'm enjoying math as
> much as I am. Gym still sucks."

I want to

tell them about Tommy   *so bad.*

I want to say,

> *There's this guy who has my stomach in knots. His*
> *smile makes me warm, and his voice feels like*
> *honey. Why honey? I don't know. Maybe because*
> *it's sweet. I think he likes me. I mean, I like him.*
> *He's really cute. And he wants to hang out with*
> *me. He even calls me beautiful. Yeah, I know he's a*
> *sophomore, but he's actually pretty cool. I think you*
> *guys would like him. I want you guys to meet him.*
> *His name is Tommy.*

But I can't.
    I don't know why,
but I can't.

            I can't do it.

            I can't tell them.

39. FOR THE FIRST TIME

When I get home,
I stand in front of the bathroom mirror and think
                        for the first time,
Maybe I am pretty.

40. THE NEXT NIGHT

I can't sleep.
I can't sleep.
I can't sleep.
     Tomorrow   I meet *Tommy*   at
       the mall   by myself.

What will we do?

   Is this—
Like—
     A date?

               Is.This.My.First.Date?
He didn't say it was a date, though.

           But is it?

41. THIS MORNING

Although

I'm getting dressed for church,

      I'm really getting dressed

            for *Tommy*.

42. I DON'T TELL MOM

That I'm not staying at church for flag practice.
She hugs me real tight.
    "Have a good rehearsal, baby."
She leaves with Mrs. Porter.
I wait a bit.

I dodge Sade and Amare.

I race my shadow to the bus stop.

I catch the bus to the mall,   hoping nobody sees me.
I pray nobody sees me.

I mistake almost every person on the bus   for Mom.
    I pray that nobody sees me.

I try to be as invisible as possible.

> My heart
> is beating
> out of
> my chest.

Although I've been to this mall so many times,
it   just doesn't feel the same.
I walk around with clumsy feet
pacing
looking around   like a tourist.
My heart racing,
my mind spinning,   constantly checking
my phone.

> *Deep breaths, Rain.*
>   I walk into different stores

pretending to shop, to browse
and
look at myself in mirrors
praying
to appear thinner and
more beautiful.

Should I text him?
I walk down to the food court,
lean against a table,
scroll down to *T* in my contacts.

"Rain!"
I hear,
but it's not yelled   it's more sung
in two syllables like
Ra-ain.
I look up and it's *Tommy.*
Oh my God.

"Hey!" I look down at his hands, which have bags in
them. "You went shopping?"

"I couldn't help myself." He smiles. "Come here,
girl."
But I don't move.
Instead
he comes up to me,   wrapping his arms around me
real tight, real close.
Hugging outside of school walls   seems so
personal,   so private,   so intense

to me.

So suffocating,   yet so warm.

He feels as soft as cotton.

He smells like a fresh shower.

After shopping—how?

My face gets hot.

I back away.

      "We can sit here," he says.

He puts his bags on the table I was leaning on.

      "Okay."

I sit down,   but he doesn't.

"Want to get something to eat? Whatever you want, I
      got you."

I like that he says,   *I got you.*

I smile, but

I don't want to eat in front of him.

I don't want to look too hungry.

Or too greedy.

      "Oh, okay."

      "Burgers? Fries? Soda?"

I don't really want that, but

      "Okay, sure."

He walks away to get it and

I can feel the sweat   on my face,

                              under my arms,

                              on my back,

dripping
d
o
w
n.

Breathe, Rain, breathe.

What will we talk about?

I scroll on my phone to distract myself.

It dings with an alert.

Rain-drop!

Xander.

I panic.

I look around me.

Oh *no*.

Is he here? Does he see me?

Did he come home for something?

I write back:

Where are you?

I keep looking around me to see if he sees me

sliding down in my seat, hiding.

It chimes again.

I can't breathe.

Leaving my dorm room. Heading to the library.

Wyd?

I exhale.

Thank God.

"You good?" I hear.

I look up to see

Tommy putting two trays down on the table.

He sits across from me,   his knees accidentally
    hitting mine.

    "Yeah, I'm good, it's just my brother."

He unwraps his burger and takes a bite.

    "Younger or older?"

    "Older." I take a bite of a french fry. "He's away at
        college."

His eyes widen as he drinks his soda.

    "That's what's up." He reaches for his shopping bags.

        "Want to see what I got?"

His smile is mischievous.

    "Yeah." I smile.

I feel giddy.

I feel happy.

I've never felt *this way* before.

I can't believe I'm really here with him.

He starts taking out some shirts   that are actually
    really nice

and look kind of *expensive* too.

    "You think these will look good on me?"

He wants to know *my* opinion.

I look away, slightly   nervous.

He'd look good in anything.

He laughs.

"I guess that's a yes?"

I laugh.

"Yes, yes, they're nice."

He puts them back inside the bag.

"So tell me about yourself?"

Myself?

"About myself?"

He stuffs fries into his mouth.

I take a small bite of my burger.

"Yeah, like what are your likes? Dislikes? Anything."

Oh.

"Oh—umm, I like school. Well, I like learning.
English is usually my strongest subject, but I
don't mind any of them, honestly. I like to write.
I used to hate math, but my teacher this year,
Ms. Familara? Ms. Fam? You heard of her? Well,
she's really cool, so I'm liking it better. Umm . . .
I like to hang out with my family. And when
I say family, I mean my older brother and my
mom. Then my friends as well. I was on a step
team last year that was really fun. And I do this
thing at church: it's like praise dance with flags.
It's cool."

He nods as I speak,   as if

I'm saying the most brilliant things in the world,

which I'm not.

He wipes his mouth and hands with a napkin.

"That's wassup, Rain. Also, *Rain*. Your name is so
dope. How'd you get it?"

Your name is so dope.

I'm   tripping   off   of   his   words.

"Oh, my mom. I was born in the springtime and—"

"—it rains a lot in the spring. I dig it, I dig it a lot."

I smile shyly and take a sip of my soda.

Then I

look over Tommy's shoulder and see

wait a minute

Umi's face   *oh*   then his eyes

my

looking   staring   at me   *God.*

But I pretend not to see,

staring down at my cup

until he's out of the food court.

Oh no, no, no, no.

"You cool?" *Tommy.*

"Yeah, I just—"

"I'm so glad you could come out and hang with me."

He bites into his second burger, and somehow

mayo and ketchup

on his chin don't make him any less handsome.

Somehow *more* handsome.

My stomach is turning.
And I can't tell if it's from being with Tommy,
    from seeing Umi,
or from the burger I'm slowly eating.
    "You are?" I'm almost whispering.
Did I just say that out loud?
He smiles.
    "Yeah—I am."
Now he's whispering and getting   *real* close,
    too close   to my face.
    "So, umm, tell me about you," I say so fast that it
        sounds like
tellmeaboutyou.
I look down at my phone to see if Umi texted me,
    but he didn't.
I know he saw me—he had to.
I feel bad about Umi,
but I also feel like I'm floating on fluffy white clouds
    with   Tommy.
Tommy leans back into his seat, thinking.
Then he starts telling me about
                    how he loves running
                        morning runs are the best
                    eating junk food and his mom's
                    cooking
                                    got to have both
                    Saturday-morning cartoons

I miss the shows I watched as a
kid
learning phrases in other
languages
me gusta aprender mucho
disliking peanut butter
it tastes so gross to me
meeting new people
especially if they're beautiful like you.

I sketch these things in my heart;   they live rent-free
there.

I can't stop smiling.

Beautiful like you,   he says.
Like me,   he means.

43. WHEN I GET HOME

Mom's already at work.
So I
go into my room and
lie down on my bed.

I'm thinking about *all   things   Tommy*.

How he makes me smile.
How he makes my stomach twist and turn.
How he hugs me.
How he listens to me.
How he says my name.
How he makes me feel pretty.
How he makes me feel warm.
How he makes me *feel*.

44. BUT THEN I REMEMBER

Umi.

45. THE NEXT DAY

During lunch
when Alyssa and I sit down   at our usual table
in the cafeteria,
Umi texts our group chat:
**I'm helping the art teacher with something, see y'all
    later**
    "So he's *not* coming?" Alyssa.
I shrug and shake my head *no.*

And I know he's avoiding us   well, *me*
because I never told him   well, *them*

that I was hanging out with Tommy,
or that I even know him.
But he can't be mad at me for meeting new people in high
      school . . .   right?

At the end of the period,
as I'm walking out of the cafeteria with Alyssa,
Tommy and his friends start walking by us.
Tommy bumps me slightly and says,
      "My bad," with a small smirk and keeps walking.
I try my hardest not to smile back.

When I get home—I text him:
Had a great time at the mall.

46. HOW I FEEL ABOUT THAT

I pray that my session with Dr. Sherif ends quickly
or that she lets me out early, but that *never*
    seems to happen.
    "How are things with your dad?" she asks.
I freeze because
I was rambling on about random things from history
    class.
What does that have to with my dad?
    "Umm—he's good, I guess."
    "You *guess*?"
Ugh—why does she always do that?
    "He's good."
    "How do you know he's good?"
    "Well, he calls."
    "And *you* speak to him?"
    "Not really, no. My mom does."
    "Is that your choice?"
    "Yes."
    "How do you feel about that?"

How do I feel about that?
I shrug.

   "It's fine."

47. IT'S TOMMY

As soon as I get home from school,
my phone vibrates and

                              it's Tommy:

Thinking about you.

48. I'VE NEVER WORN A DRESS TO SCHOOL

Outside of graduation.

But today I wear one.

An orange sweaterdress.

I want to ask Tommy if it looks nice on me.

I really want him to see me in it.

Umi is first at our lunch table, already
     eating,
meaning
he got his lunch   without   me.
     "Hey, Umi," I say with a small smile.
He looks up at me from his mozzarella sticks and nods.
     "Hey."
Alyssa sits.
     "Rain, you can have some of my lunch if you don't
          feel like going on that *crazy* line."
I look up and see Tommy at a table with some of his
     friends.
     "Uhh—yeah, sure."
As we eat,   Alyssa is talking about
another family party, but I can barely hear her
as I
watch Tommy and
as Umi
keeps looking straight into my eyes like I'm in a
confessional.
We pile our garbage onto Umi's tray.

"I'll throw it out it!" I say quickly,   maybe
        too quickly.

I organize the garbage on the tray and walk it over to
        the trash can.

On my way back to our table I purposely
walk past Tommy's table.

And   although he doesn't say anything
he raises his eyebrows at me,   at the dress.

When I sit back down,
butterflies   so many

                              butterflies
                                   swirlswirlswirl
                                        around in my
                                        stomach.

49. MY PHONE RINGS

I hear my phone ringing
                    ringing
                         ringing
                              in my head.

Ugh.

Am I dreaming?

I drag my phone from under my pillow.

"Hello?"

My eyes blurry, my voice hoarse.

"It's X, sis."

I look at the time:

2:16 a.m.

Is something wrong?

OhmyGodohmyGod

Something's wrong!

"Xander, what happened?!"

I jump up, rush to

turn the light on. My heart

racing, ready to wake Mom up,

ready to call 9-1-1.

He laughs.

"Nothing, Rain, wassup? Sorry to call so late, was

checking in. I just got in."

I think I hear a girl's voice.

Was that the voice of the girl that was with him that time?

I put my hand over my pounding chest.

"*Xander,*" I breathe. "You—you scared me."

"My bad, sis, get some sleep."

I hang up the phone without a goodbye.

Why would he scare me like that?

50. **IT MAKES ME LOOK DIFFERENT**

I sit crisscrossed
on the living room floor as Mom
oils my scalp.

"So, how's school going?"
I almost don't hear her because
my mind is replaying being at the mall with
Tommy.

I don't want to forget anything.
I want to remember everything,
except for the fact that Mom didn't know I was there
and that Umi saw me.

"It's going good."

"You know, sometimes I wish I could send you to a
private school. . . ."

"Mommy, it's fine. It's good. I like it."
It gets quiet as she
rubs more oil into my hair   with her fingers,
which soothes
my tender scalp.

"I see you've been dressing up."

Huh?

"Dressing *up*?"

"Yeah, like, caring more about how you look. Is
there, maybe, a little crush—"

I can hear the smile in her voice.

"Mom, *please*, stop. Why can't I just look nice for
me?"

It's quiet   again.

"It's almost time to take these out, huh?" She holds
some braids in her hand.

"Not *yet*."

I'm not ready to take the braids out   yet.

I like how they make me look   different.

Later that night,

when I'm in bed,   my phone rings.

Xander.

But when I look down at my phone, it says   *Tommy.*

Tommy?

Is this an accident?   A butt dial, maybe?

I answer it.

"Hello?" I whisper.

"Hey, Rain, what's up?"

"Nothing much," I whisper.

He laughs.

"You're so funny. You have a curfew?"

"Not exactly—"

There's a knock on my room door.

Mom pokes her head in.

I hold my breath.

She's dressed for work,   a night shift.

"All right, Rain, I'm heading out. Call me if you need anything. Oh, you're on the phone. Tell Alyssa I said good night. Love you."

"Love you too!"

I exhale.

I hear the front door close.

"Tommy?"

"What's up, beautiful?"

My heart sinks to my stomach.   *Beautiful.*

"That—that was just my mom."

"Oh, you live with your mom. Just your mom, or . . ."

"Just my mom."

"Oh, aiight. Same here. My pops is a complete deadbeat."

Oh.

"I understand what you mean. My dad isn't really around either."

"Really? That sucks. Yeah, you know, most people don't know that about me. Especially since a lot of people around here know my dad. He works for the school district and all that. But he doesn't *know me*. It's been pretty rough not

having a real relationship with him. I just keep
pushing, though. Be there for my mom. I know
that's a lot to share, but I feel like I can trust
you. I hope you can trust me too."

He *trusts* me.

Wow.

"I trust you too."

51. I HAVEN'T SPOKEN TO X

Since he nearly

absolutely

positively

tried to *kill* me from panic.

But he calls me as I'm getting ready for school.

"Sorry about the other night, Rain. I had just gotten
back from a party."

A party?

"You went to a *party?*"

The word   *party*   makes my throat dry up.

It makes me sick.

It makes me want to throw my phone.
It makes me want to go back to bed.

    "Yeah, I did."

    "How was it?"

    "It was aiight."

How could he go to a party when last year—
I can't even say it.
I can't even say it to him.
I want to ask him about that girl that's been around
      him   too,
but I'm not asking much anymore.
So instead I say,

    "Okay."

52. MAYBE

Tommy walks right past me in the hallway. He's with a
    group of his friends.

I thought he saw me. But maybe he didn't.

Maybe he didn't see me.

Tommy texts,
Meet me after school.

> I have so much homework,
> but I text back,
> **See u there.**

53. TOMMY ASKS ME

After school
Tommy asks me,

"Want to come hang out at my house next Monday?
The same bus you take to school, if you keep
going to Third Avenue, I can use my mom's car
and pick you up from the bus stop over there.
So instead of school, we can meet at my house.
I would say after school, but places just get so
crowded and noisy by then. And my house is
pretty comfortable. If you don't want to, it's fine.
I'd love to spend more time with you. Just the
two of us. Especially since the other night when
we got to talking about our fathers, it was so

dope. It was really nice having someone to talk to about that. It was really nice talking to you. It *is* really nice."

54. ALL I CAN THINK ABOUT IS

Tommy.
    I write his name in my notebooks,
in the notepad section of my phone,
                scribble a *T* on my wrist.
                        Tommy.

55. NO UMI

"What's going on with Umi?" Alyssa asks at lunch.
He's not here.

There's no Umi.

I think he's *still* mad at me since seeing me at the mall.

   With Tommy.

He's *dragging* it.

I shrug.

   "I don't know."

   "You want some?" She offers me half of her
         sandwich.

Suddenly I'm aware of my body and where the food will
   land.

I shake my head.

   "No thank you. I'm good."

   "You want to come over this weekend?"

   "Sure!"

When lunch is over and
I'm walking out of cafeteria,

                              Nara's eyes meet mine.

56. AT ALYSSA'S HOUSE

I want to tell her
about Tommy
because Alyssa's my closest friend.
    But he's a sophomore, and she may not understand
        why I'm hanging out with someone older.
I wish I could talk about his smell.
His smile.
How he makes me feel
        like girls do
in the movies.

But I don't.
I don't tell her.

        We watch Disney movies
          with her cousins
            instead.

   "Everyone, everyone!"
It's her uncle Ricky   walking into the living room

with two large bowls of nachos
with gooey cheese,

salsa,

ground beef.

He high-fives each of us,   always laughing,
    cracking jokes,

always cooking something delicious.

It tastes *really good*, but
    I try not to eat too much of it.

57. FOR THE FIRST TIME

Today I try using tweezers on my eyebrows for the first
    time.

Mommy knocks on the bathroom door *midpluck*.
    "Yes?"

I rub my sore eyebrows.
    "I was just on the phone with your dad. He says he's

been speaking to X."

I don't respond.

I flush the toilet instead.

58. TOMMY HAS BEEN TEXTING ME

Every day.

Hey, pretty girl.

                                        Hey!

59. THAT BLUEPRINT

Dr. Sherif is stuck on this dad thing again.

"Well, I have a good relationship with my brother," I
    protest.

"That's good. When's the last time you spoke to him?"

"Recently."

"And how was that?"

I was mad at him for nearly scaring me half to death.

"It was cool."

She nods in a way that makes me think   she doesn't
    believe me.

"And things with your mom?"

Weird.

"It's the same."

"Good, same?"

"Like—we're fine."

"And your dad, you said, *fine* as well. But you
    don't speak."

I exhale.

"Yeah, right now we don't really speak. But it's fine."

"You know, Rain. This isn't *always* true, but

sometimes young people with estranged relationships with their fathers can struggle with other relationships. Sometimes they can't tell the difference between an unhealthy versus a healthy relationship. Sometimes children miss out on that blueprint of a healthy relationship from their parents."

60. MY HEART VIBRATES

At church,
    my phone vibrates.
I look down and see that Tommy texted me three red
    heart emojis.
       My heart vibrates.
The only people that send me those are Mom and
    Xander,   and they *love* me.

                  Does Tommy—
                  Could Tommy—
                  Will Tommy—

I can't stop staring.   I'm staring
at my phone   all day.

61. I CLOSE MY EYES

I'm awake but close my eyes for a   moment
and I imagine me going downtown,
the movies,
amusement park,
mini golf,
fancy restaurant,
beachside,
lakeside,
the moon,
with *Tommy.*
I wonder where we'd get married.
My eyes jolt open.
Married?
That's too far, Rain.
But I close my eyes anyway.

And picture me in a long, flowy white dress,
Tommy in a blue tux, waiting at Hope Church's altar.
Everybody and their mommas smiling.
Xander walking me down the aisle real slow so I don't
    trip   in my
Cinderella-glass shoes.
Can't believe you're getting married, Rain-drop, he
    whispers.
There's a knock at my door.
    "Rain, dinner's ready."
I don't open my eyes.
    "Okay, Mommy."

62. I CAN'T SLEEP

It's night,   but
I can't sleep.
My head hurts.
My stomach hurts.
My heart is beating fast.
I'm sweating.
I'm so nervous.

I'm really going to   *his* house,

                          Tommy's house,   tomorrow.

And no one knows but us.

63. AS I GET READY FOR TODAY

Ready to meet up with Tommy   *at his house*

          instead of going to school,

I feel *really* nervous

              and scared.

But excited   somehow.

I put on Xander's old denim jacket over my blue-and-
     gray cropped sweater.

I use the sweetest-smelling lotion that Mom owns.

I use the sweetest-smelling spray that Mom owns.

I brush my edges with my toothbrush for the first time.

I put my hair up

              then down

then up

       then down again.

Should I tell Mommy the truth?
Or Alyssa at least?
My face and armpits are drenched   in sweat.

   "Rain, are you okay?" Mommy.
I've been sitting around the kitchen table,   barely
      eating   my cereal.
I put a spoonful in my mouth and nod.
      "Yes."   A fake smile.
      "Okay, well, you got about ten minutes." Mom
         smiles.
She doesn't *know*,   so she *smiles*.
      "Okay."

My phone vibrates.
Tommy sends me sun and cloud emojis.
I feel warm again.
I exhale.
I smile.
Relax, Rain.

Mommy hugs me before I head out the door.
She holds me real tight,
gives the kisses
and the squeezes
and the prayers.   For a second
   I wonder   if God will tell her

where I'm *really* going.
So I pray my own prayer   that   God won't   tell
        her   this once
because Tommy and I are *just hanging out.*
She lets me go.
I don't think He told her.
     "Bye, Mommy!"
     "Bye, baby!"

64. I TRIED TO IMAGINE THIS MOMENT

While I'm on the bus,   I'm so tempted
to get out at my usual stop for school,   *I even ring*
        the bell
but I don't.
I don't get off.
It feels *so weird.*
Instead
I text the group chat I'm in with Alyssa and Umi:
Not in school today.
Alyssa says:

Oh no! Are you okay?! If not, feel better.

Umi says:

Okay.

I roll my eyes at Umi's text.

I wish he'd get over it.

It's not like I   *lied.*

I just hadn't told them about Tommy   *yet.*

But today

I'll ask Tommy if

he'd like to meet them.

I think they'd like him.

I think he'd like them.

Maybe we can all have lunch together or something.

I look out the bus window   at the houses, the cars,
    the people.

The leaves changing from green to reds and browns
          reminds me

of how much things are changing in my life.

Xander crosses my mind,

          but I let that pass.

I ring the bell.

When I get out on the street that   Tommy told me to
    get out on,

my heart beats faster.

Where is he?

I look around me.

I hear the horn of a car.

"Rain!"

A white, shiny car.

His *mom's* car.

He pulls up, and I get into the front seat.

My heart starts beating even faster.

I close the door.

The car smells like pine.

He reaches over and hugs me.

"Wassup, girl!"

He smells like cologne.

His excitement shakes me up.

Should I act excited too?

"Hey!"

For the first time

I'm not sure how to feel.

I've tried to imagine this moment,   seeing him,

and now that he's here   I'm missing school.

"Welcome to the old neighborhood." He smiles.

His mom's car is real nice: leather everything,

fancy buttons,   fancy radio.

A familiar song is playing.

I can't believe that

I'm.Alone.In.A.Car.With.A.Boy.

A.Sophomore.Boy.At.That.

I don't know what to say as he drives.

    What should I say?

    "Here we are." He pulls into a driveway of a blue
        house.
When he parks,   he looks over at me.
    "You okay?" he asks.
I nod.
    "Mm-hmm."
He pushes a braid from in front of my face;
his knuckle brushes against my jaw.
    "Okay, so let's go in."
He hops out of the car and walks over to my side.
He opens the door for me.
    "Thanks," I say. I smile.
I get out of the car and look at the neighborhood.
I kind of know where I am.   My city's not that big.

Which makes me even more nervous   to be seen
    by somebody
that knows somebody   that knows me.

I follow Tommy up the steps   to the front door of
    his home.
He takes out some keys.
    "My mom and I live on the second floor."
    "Oh, okay, cool."

He opens the door   and   we walk up some steps to
     another door.
When he opens it,
there's a long hallway.
I follow him;   he makes a right.
     "This is the living room." He waves his hands in its
          direction.
It's not as fancy and shiny as the car.
It's very woody,   very brown,   very *antique*.
I walk up to this painting of a family sitting around a
     dinner table.
They're eating   and laughing.
     "That's beautiful."
     "Yeah, my mom's into art."
I think of Umi,   although I don't want to.
I notice how close Tommy is standing   and step
     away   a bit.
He goes back into the hallway,
and I follow quickly behind.
     "This is the kitchen." He stops briefly, then keeps
          walking. "Here's the bathroom, a closet, my
          mom's room, my room."
He stops.   I stop.
He opens the door and walks in.
     "How do you like it?"
I walk in, and it's way bigger than my room
and Xander's room   *combined*.

He has a bunk bed, a dresser, a desk,
	a television, beanbag chairs.
He even has a little walk-in closet.
	"Wow, your room is *huge*," I say, still looking
		around.
There's a strong cologne scent.
		The one I smelled in the car.
	"Yeah, my mom let me have the bigger room." He
		sits on the bottom bunk of his bed.
It makes me think of *my* mom, who
shares a room with me but often
	sleeps on the living room sofa. But with Xander at
		school,
Mom sleeps in his room, *if* she's not working the night
	shift.
	"That's nice of her," I almost whisper.
I stand awkwardly.
I feel awkward.
Relax, Rain, relax.
	"Want to sit?" He pats the space next to him on his
		bed.
I shake my head.
	"No, it's okay, I'm good."
I look at his wall of posters   of
rappers, singers, bands,
	athletes, colleges.
	"Basically, just about anything you see in this

room—my dad bought. I hate that. I hate how
he can just spend money on me, then disappear."
Instantly I think of Dad
and how the last time when we spent time together
was him *paying* for the movies,   then
     disappearing.
I nod.
     "I understand."
I'm still too *nervous* to sit.
He stands up.
     "Okay, Rain, so we can chill in here or in the living
          ro—"
     "The living room works!"
     "Aiight, cool."
I exhale.
Breathe, Rain, breathe.

65. IN HIS LIVING ROOM

Tommy turns on the TV,
          he puts on a funny movie,
          we laugh together.

In his living room,

        Tommy offers me apple juice,

        he gives me spicy chips,

        he makes me toss some into his
        mouth.

In his living room,

        Tommy scoots down closer to me on the
        sofa,

        he calls me beautiful,

        he hugs me but doesn't let go.

In his living room,

        Tommy puts his face too close to mine,

        he wraps his arms too tight against my
           body,

        he tries to kiss my face.

66. THE SAME GUY

I scoot away from him on the sofa.
Why is he doing this?

My heart beats fast.

He grabs the remote and turns the TV off.

He scoots closer, he moves faster,   his body
    begins to crush mine.

            He's *heavy.*

I dodge his lips.

            He's *strong.*

"Tommy!" I push him off of me and

                                jump up from the
                                sofa.

I'm breathing heavy.

My heart's beating fast.

He sits up.

He shakes his head.

"You came all the way here to watch TV? This ain't
    a movie theater."

What do you mean?

"I thought we were hanging out." My lips are
    trembling.

I'm starting to feel sick.

I want to call Mom.

I want to throw up.

"Whatever, Rain." He stands up.

Whatever?

"You—you told me—"

"Nah, I'm not trying to hear it. Don't try to act
    dumb now. *You* came to *my* house."

Tears fill my eyes.

"Yeah, I did, but I thought—"

He walks out of the living room, and I follow behind.

So far behind.

He opens the front door.

"Nah, obviously you weren't thinking. It's cool. You
can leave now, freshman."

His voice is cold   like ice.

He's never called me *freshman* before.

The way he says   *freshman*   like he's
disgusted.

Is he serious?

"Leave?"

He nods his head in the direction of the door.

OhmyGodohmyGod.

I look at him,   shocked

by this   sudden

stranger.

Is this the same guy that picked me up
from the bus stop?
The same guy from the mall?
The same guy from school?
The same guy I've been talking to on the phone?
The same guy who calls me *beautiful*?

This can't be real. It just can't be.

I step out the door and turn to him.

    "Tommy."

He slams the door right in my face.

Slams   it   in

       my   face.

I walk down the front steps,   then down the

    sidewalk,

tears

running   *racing*   down my cheeks.

67. AND THE THOUGHTS

That I had last year,

that kept me in dark clouds,

that made me feel lost,

that got worse after Xander got hurt,

that made me hurt me,

that made me feel broken,

        are now

spinning
you're not beautiful
spiraling
nobody loves you
wildly
nobody cares about you
in
you're lonely
my mind.

68. I'M WALKING

And crying,
I'm walking   and crying

trying to find this
stupid bus stop.

Why would Tommy do this?
Why would he do this to me?

The wind is making
it feel   so much colder

                                    than it was   this
                                                morning.

Why would Tommy treat me like this?
Why would he hurt me?

I'm praying no one sees me,   no one sees me
like this.
                                    I just feel so alone.
I want to call Mom, Xander, Alyssa, Umi.
          But they'd be so disappointed, so mad
                    at me.

I'm walking,
walking fast   past buildings   to
    get to the bus stop.

I think—   *my mind is in such a fog.*
I see—   *my eyes are so blurry with tears.*

Nara.

Is that Nara coming out of one of those buildings?
Is that really her?

She's not at school?

"*Rain?* Rain—what are you doing here?"

It's her.

And she's walking up to me.

Ohnonono.

I try to wipe my face,   my tears,   my snot,
        my sleeve stained with both.

"I—uh—wait, you guys *moved*?" I ask.

She shakes her head in disgust.

She crosses her arms over her chest.

        "No. My dad got an apartment in this building. My
                parents are separating, and they're just *dragging*
                this whole thing."

My eyes widen.

Separating?

Nara's parents?

They just—

        "Seemed perfect, huh?"

She reads my mind.

        "Yeah, I mean, I had no idea."

        "Yeah, you'd have to live with them to know, I guess.
                They didn't really get along. My dad's been
                staying here for a few months now."

She squints at me.

        "Wait. Rain. Are you *crying*? Are you okay?"

I can't speak.

I burst into tears,   an overflow,   a lake,   an ocean.

A *rainstorm.*

"Rain."

She comes up to me, she hugs me.

This makes it worse.

This makes me cry even more.

"Rain, what's going on? Is it Xander? Your mom?"

The tears fall so fast and so hard.

"Tommy . . . I—I went to his house—"

"His *house*? By *yourself*?"

"Yes."

A lump forms in my throat.

It hurts.

It hurts so bad.

All of this hurts.

I pull away from her to wipe my face some more.

"What happened?" Her voice is gentle.

The most gentle I've ever heard it.

"We've been talking a lot. We went to the mall, and
he invited me to his house. And I know that's
dumb of me. I know it was. But he seemed so
cool, and he wanted to hang out with me, you
know? With *me*. He seemed really nice. He
was so nice to me. Literally, the nicest person.
But he was getting all touchy, and I didn't like
that. We were watching TV, and he just started
hugging on me and wouldn't let me go. It made
me uncomfortable, so I stopped him, and he just

kicked me out like I was nothing. He didn't even look at me when I was leaving, Nara; he didn't even say goodbye."

I'm sobbing through my words.

She's nodding,   looking at me,   *through me.*

   "Firstly." She exhales. "You're not nothing. Secondly, Tommy's a jerk."

The bus I need to take home approaches the stop.

Nara says,

   "This is your bus. I'll text you, okay? You have the same number, right?"

I nod,   wiping away more tears.

I get on the bus,   pay the fare,   sit down, and continue to cry,   thinking,

Why did I do this?
Why did I do this to me?

69. WHEN I GET HOME

My phone dings.
I think, kind of hope, it's

Tommy to make sense of
all this.
But I look down   to a number   that
although *deleted*
I've had memorized as much as Mom's number
Xander's number
my address
my date of birth
my hair color.
You okay, Rain?

Nara.

70. I'M NOT OKAY

You're not beautiful.

I get into bed,   under the covers,
praying to disappear.

Nobody loves you.

X FaceTimes me, but I don't answer him.

Even when he calls the fifth time,   I just
                              can't.

                                        Nobody cares about
                                              you.

Mom asks
                if I'm hungry, but I tell her I already ate,
                      although I haven't moved from this spot.
I tell her
                I have a lot of homework *and* a test.
She says she's exhausted from work and goes into X's
      room to sleep.
                                        You're lonely.

71. THE NEXT DAY

I do *all the things*
as if I'm going to school.

I put on jeans and   one of Xander's old hoodies.

I try   my hardest   not to cry   around Mom.

I sit at the kitchen table with a yogurt.

I force myself to swallow one spoon of it.
    My stomach hurts *so bad*.

    "Rain, what happened to your eyes? They're
        swollen."
I *really* don't want to lie.
Mom comes close to me and holds my chin.
    "I left the window open and—"
    "There's a draft; I feel it too. Make sure it's closed
        tonight. Don't want you getting sick."
Too late.
I nod.
    "Okay."

I walk to the bus stop.
But I don't get on the bus.

I go back home after I know Mom is gone for sure.

I turn my phone off,
lie in bed,
and cry.

72. THE NEXT DAY

I purposely miss the bus to school.
I walk around the block a few times, eyes heavy,
    body hurting, with
dread of seeing Tommy   or anybody else.
But mostly Tommy.

                I pray I'm invisible in
                Xander's oversized
                hoodie.

I turn on my phone to see that I have a few missed calls
from
Xander and Alyssa.

When I catch the late bus,   *I pray it breaks down.*
But it doesn't.

When I get to school,
not only *don't* I see Alyssa,
but I don't see Umi.

I want to skip first-period gym,   but I can't.
I have nowhere else to go.
My legs feel like Jell-O.
I'm sweating real bad.
My stomach is in knots.
I think I'm going to vomit.

I walk into the gym and sit off to the side
since I'm not dressed.
          I don't see Tommy.
I exhale.
          Breathe, Rain, breathe.
I close my eyes and lean my head back against the wall.

73. HE'S HERE

He's here.
He's here.
He's here.
TommyishereTommyishereTommyishereTommyishere.

Why is he   here?

And who is that   girl   that   he got all up on
     him
like candy   stuck to a wrapper?

It's a girl   in this
gym class.

He bends down   and   kisses her on   the lips.

I can't. I can't. Breathe.

The gym is   starting to spin.

I run into the locker   room. I   can't feel
   my   face
or my legs
but

spinning.

I feel myself f
         alling.

74. I OPEN MY EYES

And see faces.

"Give her the water."

A woman kneeling next to me   helps me to sit up.
A girl hands me a cup of water.
   "When's the last time you ate?" the woman asks me.
   "Yesterday."
   "What'd you eat?"
   "Some yogurt?"
   "Just yogurt? And this was yesterday?"
   "I think so."
I begin sipping the water.
   "What's your name, hun?"
   "Rain. Rain Washington."
She uses a stethoscope on me.
She wraps that thing around my arm to check my blood
   pressure.
She checks my temperature.
   "Help her up."
I realize
that this woman is the school nurse.
Two girls,   one on my left,   one on my right,
   hold my arms,   my elbows.
They help me stand.
And although I feel okay to walk,
they walk me to the nurse's office anyway.
I keep my head down as we walk the halls.
I'm so embarrassed.

They bring me into this small room in the nurse's office

that has a bed in it.

They help me up on the bed.

"Thank you," I whisper.

They walk out, and I begin to cry.

The nurse walks in.

"I'm sorry." I wipe my tears.

"No, no, it's okay. How are you feeling?"

She hands me two granola bars.

She sits on a chair in front of me.

"Thank you." I open one and start eating.

I'm so hungry.

"You said you haven't eaten? How long has this been going on? Some *yogurt* on a day you don't remember—does not sound like you're eating."

"I don't have an eating disorder or anything. I just . . . I just did this."

"You ever done this thing before? Stop yourself from eating."

"I . . ."

I'm so *exhausted* and *terrified.*

I drink some more of the water from my shaky hands with shaky lips.

I don't want to get in *trouble.*

I start again.

"Sometimes my stomach hurts or I get nauseous and it's hard to eat. When—when I'm stressed

out, it happens. I—I just want to go home."
I wipe more tears from my eyes.
"I'm trying to get in contact with your mother right
now."
She walks out of the room, and
I lie all the way back on this bed
with its noisy paper sheet.
I close my eyes as the tears warm
every part of my
face.

75. IN THE CAB RIDE HOME

Mom holds me tightly.
"I'll make some soup," she whispers, "when we get
home."
"Okay," I whisper back.

76. TO SEE THEM HURTING

The next day,
Mom isn't able to call out of work,   but she calls me a
million times throughout the day.

"How are you feeling?" she asks. "Did you eat?"

"I did," I say.

And I do.

She made a *whole large pot* of chicken soup.

I lie on the sofa,   I watch TV,

I try not to cry too much.

I try not to think of Tommy too much.

Even though it's really hard not to.

When Mom gets home,   she asks again,

"How are you feeling? Did you eat?"

"I'm feeling better and yes."

I should tell Mom

about what happened

because that's what parents are for.   *I think.*

I don't know if I can,

I don't know if I'm allowed to,

I don't know what I should know,
but what I do know is that   *I can't tell her.*

She comes to sit next to me on the sofa,
so I sit up.

 "Alyssa's mom called last night. But you were
   resting."

Her mom?

 "Her mom? Why?"

Mom exhales.

 "She said that Alyssa's been trying to reach you
   because of her uncle . . . Uncle Ricky got arrested
   Monday night."

My heart drops.

 "*Arrested?!* Wait, what? *Why?*"

Wait—what did he do?

 "Arrested in the sense that they're detaining him
   because of his status in this country."

 "His *status?*"

 "Yes, because he's undocumented. Meaning,
   without legal documentation."

 "So he has to get *arrested?*"

 "Sometimes they do that when they're trying to
   deport—"

 "Deport?! Oh no, no, no!"

I get up and run into my room.

I get my phone and turn it on.

There's a text message from Umi:
The cops came for Uncle Ricky.
Oh no, no, no.
I call Umi.
"Hello?"
"Umi, what's going on with Uncle Ricky?"
"It's ridiculous. I can't believe it. My pops is bringing
me to Alyssa's house in an hour. You want to
come?"
I want to, but I'm scared to go.
I'm scared to see them hurting.
"Yes."

77. THIS IS HAPPENING TO FAMILIES

When Umi's dad picks me up,
I'm reminded that Umi and I have *beef*,　　because he
doesn't look my way.
He doesn't even say anything to me.
"Good evening, Rain." Umi's dad.
"Good evening," I say.

The drive is quiet.
I want to fix this *Umi* thing,
but my mind is blown
trying to imagine Uncle Ricky,   *one of the kindest*
     people I know,
detained.

When we get to Alyssa's house,
it's her mom that lets us in.
Her skin is pale,   drained,   eyes swollen.
     "Hello," she says.
There's no song to her greeting,   no kisses on the
     cheek,   no music when we step in,
no smell of delicious dishes.

Everyone is huddled in the living room,
holding,   crying,   praying,   yelling in
     frustration.
No celebration today.
No dancing today.
Is this the same house?
     "She's in her room," Alyssa's mom says, pointing in
          that direction.
Umi and I nod.
Umi knocks on Alyssa's room door.
     "Alyssa, it's me and Rain."
     "Come in," we hear.

When Umi opens the door,

Alyssa is on her bedroom floor, wrapped in a blanket.

"Alyssa, I'm so sorry."

I sit on the floor next to her and hold her.

Her shoulders start to shake.

Her crying hurts me so deep.

It makes the Tommy thing feel like a grain of sand in a
desert.

God, please bring Uncle Ricky back. Please.

"I don't get it," I say. "I don't."

"This isn't right," says Umi.

Alyssa sits up a bit.

"It happens. We've lived with this fear forever.
Basically, all the adults in my family are
undocumented. Even my parents."

I can't believe this.

"This is wild," I say.

"It's not easy. Uncle Ricky has been here since he
was eight years old. But it's so hard for him to
get his proper paperwork to be legal. Everyone
came here to escape struggle and violence.
They came here for a better life. He's been here
basically his whole life and gets treated like a
criminal."

Eight years old?

She cries again.

Umi gets down on one knee.

"How can we help?" he asks.

She shakes her head.

"I'm not sure. We have an immigration lawyer now.
     There's an advocacy group trying to help us too."

Huh?

"Advocacy group?" I ask.

"Yeah, a group that helps undocumented people.
     They help fight for families and for people like
     Uncle Ricky, who just wants to live, work, and
     take care of his family."

I close my eyes and imagine all of my encounters with
     Uncle Ricky.

Of him singing,   dancing,   cooking,
     cracking jokes,

holding his wife,   hugging his children.

Not detained.

Not detained for trying to give his family a better life.

I can't believe this is happening to him.

                    I can't believe this is
                         happening to families.

78. AN OCEAN BETWEEN US

Umi and I stand in front of Alyssa's house,
waiting for his dad.
It's cold—   well,   *I'm* cold.
I cross my arms over my chest.

    "Everything's cold," I say aloud, by accident.
Umi looks at me and
instantly I remember his name
also
means *water*
because it feels
like there's an *ocean*   between us.
I look down from his gaze.

    "I know you saw me," I say. "At the mall that
        time."
He's quiet.

    "And . . ." Tears fill my eyes. "It's not what you
        think."

    "What do you think I think?" His voice is harsh.
  Hurt.

I look back up at him.

"To be honest, I'm not sure. He's someone I met at
school. I thought he was nice. Well, he *was* nice,
at first. But then he turned out not to be nice at
all."

"You like him?"

"Not anymore."

His dad pulls up, and
we're quiet again.

When I get home,
I cry to Mom about Uncle Ricky.
Not just because he's detained
but because he's a *good* dad,
a *present* dad,
a dad who actually *cares*,
being taken away from his   family.

79. HUMAN

Dr. Sherif knows what happened to me during gym
     class.
I can barely look at her.
I look down at my lap   instead.
     "Rain, this isn't going to work if you're not
          honest."

So I tell her.
I tell her all about Tommy.
I tell her about all the thoughts coming back.

     "Everything was on his terms. Even just speaking to
          each other," I say.
She hands me a tissue to wipe my eyes.
     "Why didn't you tell him? Why didn't you tell
          Tommy what you needed? Your boundaries?
          Your limits?"
"I don't know."
"You *do* know, Rain. You do the same thing with

your brother. And your dad. And your mom as
well. You always say things are fine. But you
don't tell them. You don't tell them what you
need. Why do you think you do that?"

"I don't know."

"You *do* know."

I pause.

I do?

I think.

I do.

"I guess I don't want to burden anyone. I don't want
to feel crazy either."

"Crazy for having *needs*? Rain, you're human. And
every human deserves to have their needs
not only acknowledged but honored and met
because it's what's *required* by you to function as
the *best* version of yourself. Do you understand?"

I shake my head *yes.*

I hope I do.

"From what I know, your mom has sacrificed so
much. Xander does the same, right? These are
needs given up as a survival tactic. But you
don't have to be in survival mode all the time,
Rain. None of you have to. And you have to be
intentional about that."

I nod. *She's right.*

I think of Uncle Ricky.

"But now, there's this whole thing with Alyssa's
uncle. And I wasn't even honest with her or
Umi about Tommy. And now her uncle Ricky
is detained. It's just so much at once. I thought
because of Xander's incident, stuff like this
should be no big deal. Like I should be able to
handle hard stuff better."

"Rain, experiencing trauma does *not* mean the
absence of feeling the weight of hard times or
future struggle. And I know Umi and Alyssa,
and I know they care about you very much. True
friendship can withstand a few hiccups and
changes along the way. Again, you are *human*."

I nod.

She's right.

I'm *human*.

We all are.

When I leave Dr. Sherif's office,
Umi sends a text to our group chat:
Hey, guys. Meet me in the art room during lunch.

80. SOME TABLES HAVE BEEN MOVED

When I meet up with Alyssa to   meet with Umi
in the art room,
I can tell she's been crying.
Her face is red,   her eyes small.
   "You okay?" I ask, although I already know the
      answer.
Why did I even ask that?
She nods her head *yes* anyway.
I link my arm with hers and we walk there.

When we get to the art room,
some tables have been moved.
            We see Umi   sitting on a stool in the
               middle of the room.
On each of his sides, two other stools.
I breathe out,
"Circle Group."

81. ROSES AND THORNS

Umi, Alyssa, and me,   just the three of us,
sitting in our own   little   Circle Group
in the art room.

We sit quiet for a while,
 a comforting concept   feeling so   unfamiliar.
            "So . . ." Umi plays with his hands. "Roses
                    and thorns of the day."
I don't know where to start.
It's been hard to divide the good from the bad
      lately.
I look at Alyssa,   who looks at Umi,
who looks down at his lap.
      "Okay. I'll go first," he says.
I exhale.
He claps his hands together.
He looks up.
      "My rose is . . . I guess my rose is right now. And my
            thorn . . ."
He looks at Alyssa.

"Uncle Ricky," she says.

He nods.

"Yeah, Uncle Ricky," he agrees.

She exhales.

"My thorn is Uncle Ricky." She wipes her eyes. "My
rose is that he's holding up. He's hopeful. And
I'm grateful although we hate being without
him."

Umi and I nod.

I don't get

how a *good* man

who's been living here longer than

I have been *alive*   can be a criminal   for *living.*

"Well." I look down at my hands. "Like Umi, my
rose is right now."

I look up at him.

He nods for me to continue.

"Umm, my thorn is Uncle Ricky. But also, the fact
that I haven't been honest with you guys is a
pretty big thorn for me."

"Honest about what?" Alyssa puts her hand on my
shoulder.

"About a guy."

"A guy? Like a *guy*?" Alyssa.

I nod.

Her eyes widen.

I exhale.

Here we go.

"Yeah—well, there was this guy who would pop into my gym class. He would, like, talk to me and just say really nice things. We started talking more and became cool. I thought he liked me or something. I guess, to be honest, I started liking him too. He . . . he's a sophomore. Which I know sounds crazy, but he just seemed really cool at the time. Anyways, we hung out at the mall once. Umi saw us. I saw him too but didn't say anything. So that's why the group became awkward. I wasn't telling you guys about him, and he saw us. Oh, his name is Tommy, by the way. So anyway, he . . . invited me to his house. And . . . and I went . . ."

"Oh *no*." Alyssa.

"And—" I clear my throat. "It was okay at first, but then he started getting touchy and—and I was freaking out. And I basically pushed him away from me and he literally just told me to *get out*. It was bad. I was crying. I was trying to find the bus stop to get home. I ran into Nara, and she talked me through it a bit. But for a few days I wasn't really eating and I was feeling really sick. And then when I saw him in gym class again, he was kissing some girl and it . . . it was bad. I basically passed out in the locker room from everything. I got sent home. That's why I was missing school. And that's why I missed the calls about Uncle Ricky. And I feel terrible that I haven't been as present as I should've been because of this Tommy mess."

Alyssa gets up and hugs me.

"Oh my *God*, Rain. *That's so crazy.*"

"Wait—did you tell your brother? Your mom? The *school*?" Umi. His hands fisted.

"No, no, no! My mom would kill me, and my brother would kill *him*. They'd both kill him. Not for real, but . . . actually, I'm not so sure about Xander. And no, the school doesn't know. I mean, besides Dr. Sherif—"

"Rain, stop, wait." Umi's voice rises. "So you're telling me that kid is walking around like what he did to you was okay?"

"*Umi.*"

He shakes his head.

"I swear, if I see that kid, it's over."

"Umi, *please*, it's okay. Don't do anything, please."

"It's *okay*, Rain? What he did to you was *okay*?"

The bell rings.

82. NOT IN THE GOOD WAY

The next morning,
Alyssa, Umi, and I are   standing at our
    lockers.
The hallway, *per usual,*   is loud   and
    crowded.

"You did the math homework?" Alyssa asks me.

"Yeah, for once, I knew what I was doing. Ms. Fam
    is the best."

"Seriously."

"Y'all lucky y'all have her," says Umi. "My math
        teacher is the oldest man to walk the earth. I'm
        talking, took his first steps during the Ice Age."

We laugh.

I look over my shoulder and see Tommy.

I turn my head quickly,   basically hiding my face
in my locker.

"Is that him?" Umi.

"Umi, you're talking *way too loud,*" I whisper.

There are so many people standing around Tommy,
there's no way he can know who he is.

"The one in the green hoodie?" Umi whispers.

My heart drops.

He *is* in the green hoodie.

"Umi, *please*."

When I turn back around,   it's too late.

"Yo, what's good with you? You disrespecting my
      friend?"

Tommy looks confused.

"What?"

Umi points in my direction, and Tommy and I,
   for the first time in a long time,

make eye contact.

My stomach knots,   my heart races,   but
   not in the good way.

Tommy laughs.

His friends laugh.

"Get out my face with all that. Nobody told that *hoe*
      to come over to my house."

Did he just call me—

Tommy starts walking off with his friends,   but
   Umi gets in front of him and

shoves him into a wall.

Tommy shoves back. Umi punches him in the face.

Tommy punches back.

"Umi!"

I'm screaming.   Alyssa's screaming.

We're running.   Everyone's running.

No!

Phones are out.

People are fighting to break it up.

83. THIS ISN'T LIKE LAST TIME

Umi is getting suspended.

Alyssa had to head home,
but I'm still standing outside waiting for Umi.

Why would he do that?
Why couldn't he just ignore Tommy like I do?
Why did he have to go fight him?

My whole body's shaking.
I sit down on the sidewalk.

I see Tommy walk out with a woman.
His *mother.*
They're walking to the parking lot.
This time I don't look away.

I look right at him,   and when he sees me seeing him,
he looks away.

"Rain?"
I look behind me.
Umi is walking with his dad,   who doesn't look
     too happy.
     "Meet you at the car?" says Umi.
His dad nods.   I wave.
He waves back.
A man of few   *or no*   words.
Umi sits down next to me.
     "You need a ride?" he asks.
I shake my head.
     "No, I need a long walk after today." I turn to him.
          "Why would you *do that*?"
He shrugs.
     "Somebody had to."
He smiles.
I shove him.
     "Umi!"
     "Don't worry, I didn't say anything about why I did
          it either. This isn't like last time."
My mind flashes back to last year,   when Umi told
Dr. McCalla about me hurting myself.
One of the scariest days   of my life,
                              which helped

save my life.

I sit there quiet,
  embarrassed,
    sad.

"How do you feel?" he asks.

"I should be asking *you*. You got suspended, and it's
 all my fault."

It's quiet.

"Rain, I really wish you could see yourself the way
 everybody sees you."

"Like how Tommy saw me?"

"He's irrelevant. Tommy's a bozo. There's a lot of
 those out there."

I put my head on his shoulder and just

breathe.

84. WHEN I GET HOME

Mom isn't back yet.
I go into my room and

lie down in bed.

Today was   *too much.*

     I close my eyes.

My phone vibrates.

I check it.

It's Alyssa in the group chat:

#FreeUmi

I laugh out loud.

I write back:

LOL #FreeThatMan

Umi:

Y'all crazy

     I close my eyes.

My phone vibrates again.

I check my phone again.

It's Nara:

**Hey, Rain, how've you been since . . . he who should not
 be named?**

     Much better. Thank you.

I heard Umi went Mayweather on him.

     LOL he for sure did smh

Imma look if a video is out yet!

I shake my head.

Nara *still* loves the drama.

     I close my eyes.

I hear the doorbell.

Who could that be?

I wait awhile   to see if they   disappear.

Now there's knocking.

The landlord?

The doorbell again.

Ugh.

Did Mommy forget her keys?

I look at the time on my phone.   Four fifteen p.m.

Mom doesn't get off until six.

The doorbell is now ringing crazily.

What the—

I get up and go into the living room, walking real soft.

I hear keys.

    "Mommy?"

The door unlocks   and swings open.

Xander.

85. GOOD TEARS COME

"Xander!"

I jump on him,   I scream,   I cry.

"Rain-drop!"

I hold him real tight, so tight.

I never want to let go.

Is this real?

"Oh my *God*, Xander, you almost gave me a heart
attack!" I wipe the tears from my eyes.

I'm on cloud nine.

I'm in heaven.

This can't be real. This can't be real.

"Why are you here?! Does Mommy know?!"

He laughs.

"She does, she does."

He brings in his duffel bag and closes the front door.

Wait.

I grab his right ear.

"You got your *ear* pierced?!"

He turns his head to the other side.

"*Both* ears pierced?!"

"*Shhh*, where's Ma?"

"She's not here yet!"

He walks over to the sofa and throws himself on it.

"I'm beat."

"Wait." I sit beside him. "How come you're back?
There's a holiday?"

"Nope. I came back because of you."

Me?

"Me?"

"Yeah, because obviously there's beef."

"Beef how?"

"Rain, I can *never* get to you. Ever. What's up with
that?"

Is he serious?

"What are you talking about? *You're* the one that's
unreachable."

He puts his hands up in surrender.

"I'm not trying to argue or nothing. You're right.
I've been terrible. But anytime we *did* speak, you
always seemed angry with me. Listen, Ma called
me. Telling me about how you fainted at school
and all that. I'm calling you down. Nothing, no
answer. Come on, Rain. That's not *us*. What
happened? What's going on with you?"

He's looking me straight in my eyes.

My eyes water.

"There was this boy . . ." I speak slowly and softly.

"Which boy? *Umi?*"

"No, another boy. A sophomore."

"He was bullying you?!"

"No." I exhale. "We . . . we're cool and started
talking a lot. We hung out at the mall. He
invited me to his house, and it went bad."

Tears fall down my face.

Xander jumps up out the sofa.

"Wait—what?! You went to his house?! What

happened?! Did he—"

"No, Xander, no! Nothing happened! I stopped him
from getting too touchy, and he just kicked me
out!"

"Rain, why the hell would you go to his house
alone? Are you crazy? Do you know what
could've happened to you?!"

"I know." I cry.

"Who is he?! Where does he live?! Does Ma know?!"

"She doesn't! And no, *please*, Xander, it's fine now!
Please. I'm sorry!"

He sits back down.

"Rain, you don't have be sorry. I'm mad, though! I'm
mad that you went! I'm mad that I wasn't here
to protect you. I'm mad that you didn't tell me.
Rain, you can't do stuff that like that. Not *alone*.
And you said he's a *sophomore*?"

I nod.

"Rain." He rubs his hands over his face. "You know
I'll go beat him up right now."

"Umi fought him already."

"He did? I knew I liked that kid. But, Rain, really.
Why did you think that was okay?"

I exhale.

I look down.

"I don't know."

It's quiet.

"Rain, if this is that insecurity, low-self-esteem type
        stuff, listen . . . Look at me."
I look at him.
"Rain, you're better than that. You're beautiful.
        You're smart. No matter what people say. No
        matter what *you* say. Let people *earn* your trust.
        Let people *earn* your love. Listen, you got me
        out here sounding like somebody's grandfather,
        but it's true. I've seen people throw themselves
        around because their self-value is on low, and
        Rain, you're too expensive for that crap. I don't
        want to see you like one of those people. It's
        okay to be down sometimes but not to treat
        yourself like this. You got people rooting for you,
        you feel me? I'm not watching you go down like
        that, sis. And I know you want me to chill, but
        if I see that dude, it's *on sight*, sorry not sorry.
        Come here."
I lean in,   and he holds me tight.
And it feels like
        ChristmasThanksgivingFourthofJuly.
It feels like I got my
                Little Dad   back.
The front door opens.
        "Rain?"
Xander stands up.
        "Ma!"

180

"Xander!"

She runs to him,   squeezing the life out of him
like I did.

"You pierced your ears?"
She starts hitting him on the shoulder.
And I start laughing so hard,

                        and the

                                good tears come

                                        this time.

86. TODAY IS FOR US

Although Mom has to get to work early today,
she *refuses* to go
without making a big breakfast   because
all of her babies are home.
As if she had a house full of kids   who left   and
    came back.
Only X *left* left,   but
maybe   in some ways   I was a little gone
    too.

Xander and I sit around the kitchen table as she fills
    our plates with
eggs, bacon, pancakes.
When I take a bite of it,   food hasn't tasted
    this good in a long time.
I know it's more than the food;   I know it's us
    together   again.
    "Okay, okay, I have to go." Mom drops whatever's in
        her hands into the sink.
She comes and kisses X and me on our cheeks.
She opens the front door.
    "Have a good day, my babies." She looks at X. "And
        be safe."
She leaves,   closing the door behind her.
    "Be safe about *what*?" I ask, biting on a crunchy
        piece of bacon.
    "Aah." He smiles. "We're going somewhere."
What?
I notice that he's dressed.
    "Where?"
    "You'll see. After breakfast, get dressed, then we'll
        head out."
I don't really want to go   anywhere.
I just rather us stay home and hang out
before he leaves on Monday.
He reads the concern on my face.
    "Don't worry, sis," he says. "Today is for us."

87. TIME DOES WHAT TIME DOES

Xander and I are on a train,
    the *fancy* train that he used to take to high school,
        the infamous
Elite Preparatory Academy,   every morning.
I look over at X as he uses his cell phone,   chilling,
    like this is just a normal trip for us.
I look out the window to see suburbs on top of suburbs.
We've been on this train for *too* long.
I exhale.
    "Where did you say we're going again?"
This is about my fifth time asking,   to no avail.
He gently hits me on my head.
    "I *didn't* say. You'll see. Lord, you ain't got *no*
        patience, huh?"
I roll my eyes.
I try to get comfortable like him,   but I *do* notice
    that not a lot of people
on this train   look like us.
I take my phone out.
I text the group chat with Alyssa and Umi:

Xander's home!!!!!

Alyssa:

OMG!! Hi, Xander!!

Umi:

The man, the myth, the legend!

Xander shakes my shoulder.

"This is our stop."

"Finally."

When we get off the train,   we stand in the parking lot
area,   and
I'm seeing a lot of nothing.   Well, actually,
a lot of something,   that is: trees.
Now what?

"Did somebody need a taxi?" I hear.

I look to the left of me and see somebody getting out of
a car.

Tall,

blond hair.

Wait.

Zach?

"Zach!"

I run up to him and hug him.

I can't remember the last time I've hugged Zach,
if ever—

probably *never.*

I never had to.

Especially after Xander's incident.   I was
so mad at Zach for leaving X when he got hurt
by people that looked like *him*.
But it's been so long that I actually   miss him,   or
miss normal,
my heart so hungry   for normal that

> *holding on to anger*
> *would just hurt*
> *too much.*

"What's up, Rain? X, my guy." He does a handshake
   with Xander.
"What are you doing here?" I ask.
"Well." He smiles. "I live around here. And X told me
   he needed a ride somewhere."
"You have a *car*?"
"Yes, ma'am. My school is about an hour away, so
   I'm always driving back down here."
And then I notice that he has a mustache-beard thing
   going on.
Time has really changed things.
Sometimes I wish   time   could stay still.
But then I'm glad that it doesn't, because
not every moment is worth   the stillness.
Especially if there's hurt   or pain   involved.
So I guess it's better that   time does what
   time does.

"All right, so let's go!" Xander claps his hands together.

88. REMEMBER RAIN

We're at a lake.

A real-life lake.

Like   a body of water that's   not a pool.

 "What is this place?" My face pressed against the
   window.

I've never been to a lake before.

   I've never *needed* to be at a lake before.

 "Zach's parents would bring us here sometimes to
   chill. I thought you'd like it."

 "I think she'll like it," says Zach.

He parks in a little lot where a few kids are
   riding bikes and rollerblading.

 "*Oh*, I should've brought a bike for Rain!" Zach.

I think back to the time I learned to ride a bike   at his
   house.

I haven't ridden one since and

I *do not* want to injure my legs, arms, or
   anything else.

I wave my hands.

 "No, no, no, I'm good."

We all laugh.

X and I get out of the car,   but Zach doesn't
     move.

"Zach isn't staying?" I ask.

"I told you today is for us, Rain-drop!"

I wave at Zach as he drives off.

As we walk,

the trees are so colorful;   leaves *crunch* underneath
     my feet.

I'm silenced by how beautiful everything is.

The browns,   the greens,   the reds,   the oranges.

How still.

How untouched.

How *nature*.

My mouth stuck in *wow* form.

Xander's smile at my approval.

I feel calm.

I feel like there's more *oxygen* here.

I feel like I'm caught in a painting   so surreal,
     so larger-than-life.

We walk over a small bridge   to a place with
     benches overlooking the lake.

Even the chilliness of fall adds a beautiful element,
          the leaves

blowing,   twirling   magically in the air.

I guess not all change is bad change.

"How do you like it?" X.

"It's *crazy*."

He laughs.

"Yeah, Zach's parents would really have us kickin' it here on some fairy-tale stuff."

We both sit down on the bench.

"I wish life stayed this beautiful all the time."

He looks over at me.

"Life *is* beautiful."

I pause.

"Well, not for Alyssa's family right now."

"Yeah, Ma told me about that. It sucks, man. I hate that it's happening."

I sigh.

"Me too."

He gathers some leaves in his hands from the benches.

He gives some to me.

"We've had a hell of year, Rain-drop. It's foolish to think things will be perfect, but things don't need to be perfect to be beautiful."

I rub my fingers across the veins of the leaves.

"I know."

"You know, I had a breakdown at school." He laughs.

Why is he laughing?

"Xander . . ."

"No, no, I'm laughing because you wouldn't believe
     it."
"Xander."
     The way he's laughing   is about to make me
        laugh,
but I don't want to laugh at this.
     "No, no, it happened because it started raining. . . ."
     Now we're both laughing.
     "What do you mean? Like because *I'm* Rain?"
     "Exactly." He throws the leaves he has in his hands
        on the ground. "You told your truth yesterday,
        so I'll tell mine. College freaked me out—heavy."
     "It *did*?"
     "*Did it.* That night I called you? After going to that
        party?"
I nod.
     "I was freaking out. I was having panic attacks. It
        reminded me too much of—you know. I guess
        it was too soon to be doing the partying thing.
        Even just going out sometimes was a bit much.
        I remember sitting up in my room and it was
        raining, and I was down bad. I felt like I was
        failing you. I just couldn't keep up with both
        worlds."
     "Wow."
So he was struggling too.

He shakes his head.

In that moment,   for some reason,

I think about what Dr. Sherif said,   about me

expressing my needs more.

"Xander, I need you to call me back if I call you. No
matter what. Like in the same day. No excuses."

I just say it.

I just say it without overthinking it.

"Okay," he says. "And I need you to do the same."

"Okay."

I look over into the lake   and see some people
dipping their hands into it.

"Oh, you remember my therapist, who had me
playing games?" X asks.

"Yeah. He became a national Uno champ?"

I pick up red leaves and hand him some.

He laughs.

"Nah. He kept at it, though. I finally asked him
what was up. And he said, 'I want you to
remember who you are when things are
different.' That's why he would ask me what
I liked. So I can remember those things in
distress. As an outlet. As little pockets of
happiness. As a reminder of me. Yeah, I don't
play sports seriously anymore, but football was
a stress relief, so I can go throw a ball around
if I need to. I can remember me. Not only the

me that came through trauma, but the *real me*.
And you can do the same, Rain. When things
change, you have to remember you. Find your
little pockets of happiness. Find your little
outlets. You have to remember *Rain*."

I nod.

I never thought about that before.

I knew I had to *remember* my truths   but never
      thought about *practicing* them.

But I guess that makes sense.

One needs to go with the other.

How'd he get so deep?

X stands up,   clapping his hands together.

      "Aiight. Let's go find some leaf piles to jump in."

There he is.

On the train ride back home,
          I look over at X,
hoping he'll be okay once he gets back to school.
          I hope he will be.
          I *know* he will be.
              Because
        in the middle of change

he will remember   *him*,   Xander,

and I will remember   *me*,   Rain.

89. GIFTS ARE TWOFOLD

At church
everyone is fawning over the prodigal son
    by way of college,

                            Xander.

X and I sit where we usually sit,
how we usually sit.
He says his usual
    "Stay awake or I tell Ma."
I laugh like I usually laugh.

    "See you at home!" I say.
X waves to me as he leaves with Mom.
I stay back for flag practice.

It's been a while.

In the practice room,
it's me, Amare, and a few others.
Sade isn't here yet.

Amare gives me a look,   and *I get it.*

I've been ghosting practice.

"Welcome back," he says. "You okay? I heard you
were sick or something."

He hands me one of my favorite flags to use.

"Yeah, I'm good now." I unravel it.

It's shimmery fluorescent blue, flowing beautifully.

"At school it looks like you've been going through
it," he says.

I shrug.

"Kind of. Are we still practicing the choreography
from last time?"

He puts his hand on his chin, thinking.

We're not?

"*What?* We're not doing that one anymore?"

"We are." He pauses. "I have a question."

Oh God.

Is this about Tommy?

Did he hear?

Does he know?

"Yeah . . ."

"What do people say to you after you perform with
the flags?"

"Umm—I guess they say that it was *beautiful* . . .
or they were *touched* by it. That it made them
happy or something."

"That's cool. You're good. *Really* good, actually.

What Sade taught me, though, is that your gift
is only as good as the amount of good it can
bring to you. She says gifts are twofold."

"Yeah, I think I heard her say that before."

"Yeah, that means that if people felt happy or were
touched—your gift can do that for you too. You
know how, like, people write love poems? They
should be able to write one to themselves too,
when they need to."

"*Oh*, so you're writing *love poems* to *Brenda*, huh?"

He laughs.

"That's not what I *said*."

We both laugh.

"Yeah, okay," I say. "But no, I think I understand
what you mean."

I think of what Xander said about finding little pockets
of happiness,

about finding little outlets,

about remembering me, *Rain*.

I think this is similar to that.

"You should take the flag with you after practice,"
Amare says. "Take it home."

90. WHEN I GET HOME

It feels like some kind of

    Way Back Wednesday   Throwback Thursday

    Flashback Friday   Some Time Ago Sunday

because

Butter has a college football game that we're all tuned
    in for.

The TV is on and up   real loud.

Jay, Dre Dre, and Zach are on FaceTime with Xander.

Everyone at their own schools,   in their own
    dorms.

Their voices loud and excited.

        Their voices that will forever feel like home.

I sit on the sofa next to X,   poke my head into his
    phone.

    "Wassup, Rain!" Dre Dre.

    "Yo, Rain, what's good?" Jay.

    "Rain, what's for dinner?" Zach.

I look behind me at Mom in the kitchen.

I wave at them.

    "Chicken and rice," I say. "Everyone's invited!"

"Yeah, somebody get Zach some *seasoned* chicken!"
Dre Dre.

We're all laughing.

"You're wrong for that!" Zach laughs.
Mom walks over and sticks her head into the camera.
"Zach's mom is a great cook." She winks.

We're still laughing.

"Okay, Butter, I see you!" X.
"I see you, Butter!" Jay.
"You got this, my guy!" Dre Dre.
"Let's *go*!" Zach.
Watching Butter   lined up on the green field   in
his uniform
is so surreal.
He's one of the defensive linemen,   one of the
     ones who work to prevent the other team
                                        from scoring.
Basically   a protector of the team.
The same way I feel so   protective of this
     moment.
I never want it to end.

We're all cheering.

I've missed this so much.
Xander sitting on my left,   Mom sitting on my right.
I feel so happy,   so warm.
The warmth I was looking for was right
     here all along.

                    We're still cheering.

I feel someone shake my shoulder.
Huh?
I open my eyes slightly.
     "Xander?"
     "Yes, sleepyhead. I'm about to head out."
     "Already?" I yawn.
     "Yeah, got to take the train downtown to catch my
          bus."
     "Okay."
I sit up and hug him.
     "And, look, I promise not to break my promise and
          call you. Don't forget what we talked about,
          aiight?"
Tears wet my eyes.
     "Okay."
     "Okay, Rain-drop, gotta go. Love you."
     "Love you too, X."

91. START ONE HERE

When I wake up,
I walk up to Xander's room,   open the door,
          and it's true,
he did leave.
He's left for school.
It wasn't a dream.

At school,   *to be honest*,
I'm feeling a bit lonely.
Alyssa is home watching her cousins
          while her family meets with Uncle Ricky's
                    lawyer,   and
Umi is suspended   still.

Today I get dressed for gym,   but in the
     bathroom,   *not* the locker room.
We're still playing volleyball.
Coach Fisher is showing us the proper technique of
serving,   passing,   setting,

hitting,   blocking,   digging.
And
it's actually kind of fun today.
I look around and there's   no sign of Tommy.
Thank God.
                But then   I remember
that he must be suspended   too.

I hand in my homework for all of my classes.
Miss Fam hands me back an old assignment and says,
        "Good job, Rain."
I got everything correct   *in math.*
        Math.
I send a picture of it to X.
He texts back immediately:
That's what I'm talking about!!!! Call you tonight.

After class
I head to my meeting with Dr. Sherif.
I can't wait to tell her about me telling my needs to
        Xander.

When I get to her office,   her door is locked.
I knock but nothing.
I put my ear to the door.
Is she running late?

"Rain?"

I turn around and see Dr. Sherif, but she's standing
     with—

Miss Walia?

                              I blink hard.

It's her.

It's really her.

I can't believe it.

     "Miss Walia!"

I run up to her and squeeze her so tight.

What is she doing here?

Dr. Sherif opens the office door, and we walk in.

     "What are you doing here?!" I ask.

All three of us sit down.

     "Well, I reached out to Dr. Sherif to check in on you
          and plan a visit on my lunch break."

     "Alyssa and Umi aren't here, though . . ."

     "That's okay. I wanted to come and see *you*, Rain."

I look at her,

then at Dr. Sherif,

then back at her.

     "Dr. Sherif told you I've been a mess, huh?"

She laughs.

     "Actually, she didn't. It just seemed like time."

"Well, then *I'll* tell you. It's been kind of hard
adjusting to new things, new people."
She looks me directly in my eyes.
"Rain, you know I'm still alive, right? I'm still here.
Just across the city at the middle school."
"I know, but—"
She lifts her hand.
"I'm still here." She pauses. "Have you been
journaling?"
I can't remember the last time I journaled.
I don't even know where the one she gave me is.
"I haven't."
"Was journaling helpful for you?" Dr. Sherif.
I look at her and nod.
"It was. It helped me to get some thoughts out."
They both nod.
"I miss Circle Group, a lot," I say.
"Why don't you start one here?" Miss Walia.
I look at her.
Me?
"Me?"
"Yes!"
She claps her hands together excitedly, although
I'm not as excited.
"All you need is a staff member to be an adviser."
Dr. Sherif. "Unfortunately, after school I'm

unavailable, but I will ask around for sure."
"Think about it, Rain." Miss Walia. "Really think
    about it."

Amare waves at me when I walk into the cafeteria.
    "Where's your crew?" he asks.
    "They're both out today."
He looks over at Brenda.
She nods.
    "We can sit with you. We'll get our stuff and be
        right over," he says.
I smile.
    "Okay, cool."

While I'm eating,
I can barely hear what Amare and Brenda are saying.
I can barely taste the nuggets;
                        instead
my mind keeps replaying what Miss Walia said:
    to start Circle Group here.
Start one here?
Should I?
Could I?

92. JOURNAL

It's been a long time since I've written in this, but I'm trying to do this thing where I remember myself. Remember the things that help me. There have been a few things I'm not too proud of, but I'm doing much better. I'm not broken. I'm not nothing. I can actually try to enjoy life. It's hard sometimes, especially without X around, but I'm trying. I'm grateful for those that I do have around. I'm still learning. I'll just keep going.

93. I TEXT THE GROUP CHAT

I text the group chat with Alyssa and Umi:

What y'all think about starting a Circle Group at the High?

I wait awhile.

Alyssa:
I'm down!

Umi:
Sign me up!!

94. STAND WITH THEM

Umi is back.

When Alyssa and I see him walking into the school
building, we
cheer and clap.
We make a whole lot of noise, as if
he's an Olympian who made it back home with the
    gold,
        a soldier who made it back home from the war.
    "Okay, okay, you guys can stop now." He smiles.

During lunch,
Umi designs a flyer for us   to get a *faculty adviser*
for the *new* Circle Group.

Dr. Sherif makes copies of the flyers in her office.

We put the flyers in teachers' mailboxes,
in offices,
hang some in the hallways.

As Alyssa, Umi, and I walk home from school,
Alyssa says,
 "The advocacy group helping Uncle Ricky is holding
  a rally downtown. Like a protest. This weekend.
  They're protesting the deportations that are
  breaking families apart. Would you both be
  interested in going? My whole family is going."
I immediately think of   Martin Luther King Jr.
        Gandhi.
        Malala.
I think of human rights,
    of civil rights.
I've never been to a protest before,   and *to be honest I'm*
 nervous about it.

       Will there be officers trying
        to stop it?

Will more people get taken
away by these officers?

But
the *least* I can do is stand for them, stand
with them.

So I say,
    "Of course."

95. THE ADMIRABLE THING

Mom is packing a bag of things for me for the rally,
            the protest.
    "I put some waters in there. I also got you some
        granola bars."
Mom shuffles the house in a panic.
I feel her, though.   I'm nervous too. I wish she could
    come with me.
I wish Mommy could come with me.
    "Tell me again how you're getting downtown."
This is my third time telling her.
    "Umi's dad is dropping us at the train station, and

we'll meet Nara's family there. Then we're *all*
    taking the train to the rally."
She nods.

    "Okay, for how many hours?"
    "I think it's twelve to three."
She puts the rest of the granola bars in my bag.

    "You can share these."
I laugh.

    "Thanks, Mommy. I'm sure we'll be okay."
She nods.

    "You'll be all right. You all will." She holds my
    shoulders. "You're doing a good thing, Rain. The
    admirable thing."
She hugs me, kisses my cheek,
pushes some hair out of my face.
A car's horn honks outside.   *Umi's dad.*

96. RALLY

When we get downtown to the rally site,
    there are a lot of people.
Hundreds of people.

People not only on the sidewalks,   but pouring into
    the streets.

People of all races,   faces, and ages.
People with posters, bullhorns,   matching T-shirts.

Alyssa's mom grabs my hand and Umi's too.
    "I'm so glad you guys made it," she says.

Alyssa's siblings,   cousins,   aunts and uncles
    are all here.
Seeing Uncle's Ricky face on the posters they hold
    sends a chill throughout my body.

It makes me sad.
It makes me sick.

It makes me want to close my eyes, click the heels of
    my shoes,
    in hopes *he* finds home again.
I can imagine Uncle Ricky here,   all-loving,
    all-defending
for families,   his own   and others.

I can imagine him   *here*   with the people he loves,

                                            that love him,

not detained without them.

Someone starts speaking through one of those
bullhorns.
"Today, we are here as a voice for the voiceless
families being broken apart by deportations!
Today we stand in compassion with them!
Today we march in their honor!"

A voice for the voiceless.
Stand in compassion with them.

As we march, there are calls and responses,
cheers and chants.

"Education, not deportation!"
"When I say 'families,' you say 'together'! Families!
Together! Families! Together!"
People stare at us,   some clap,   some say negative
things,   some record us,
some get out of our way,   some get *in* our way,
but we march on.

The longer we march,   the lower my anxiety.
The longer we march,   the bigger my hope.

At first we were all strangers;

now we feel like family.

We all stop at a building, and
 a group of people walk to the top of the front steps.

"Those are the DREAMers," Alyssa says to us with
bright eyes.
"DREAMers?" I ask.

One of them starts to speak:
"We are DREAMers, fighting for our education and
to obtain careers in a country that we've been
raised in and call our home. We fight for our
dreams and for our families. Before we bring
our speakers up for today, we ask that we all link
hands in solidarity for those negatively impacted
by deportations. We do this in community, to let
everyone know they're not alone."

We all link arms.
And when each speaker comes up,
my face floods with tears,   my heart sore.

They tell their stories of the pain,   the hurting,
the missing   of family members.
I could never imagine losing

Mom or Xander   this way.

Their stories could've easily been *my* story.
I link my arms tighter with those around me.
    I will never let go of this moment.

97. WHEN I GET HOME FROM THE RALLY

I find Mom and hug her

      so

         so

            so

               tight.

98. JOURNAL

I pray and hope that I'm not one of those people
that forgets to appreciate the good people and
the good things that I have, before I don't have
them anymore.

99. AFTER CHURCH

Mom goes to work,
    and I stay in Xander's room to do my homework.
I FaceTime him.
    "What's good, Rain-drop?"
He's walking on campus   somewhere.
    "Hey, X."
I smile,

grateful that he was able to answer.

"Is that my room you're in? Y'all kicking me out
        already? I figured it would happen eventually."

I laugh.

"No, we're not!"

He laughs.

"Okay, so since you're there, smell the socks I left
        and see if they're clean."

"You're *gross!*"

He laughs some more.

"So, what are you up to?" he asks.

"Nothing much, just doing some homework."

"Okay, good. Dad actually called me earlier, and I
        was speaking to him for a bit."

Oh.

"Oh."

"Yeah—umm—how was the rally?"

"Sad, happy, but mainly sad. I can't believe people
        are going through that. Now I want to do
        anything I can to help."

"Yeah, it's tough, but I'm proud of you for
        supporting."

"Oh, by the way, Alyssa, Umi, and I are trying to
        start a Circle Group at the High."

"That's what's up!" He pauses. "That older kid's not
        messing with you still, right? I don't want to
        have to come over there."

His background becomes noisy.

He's in the dining hall.

I see that girl next to him   that I've seen before.

"He's not, he's not."

"Better not be. Rain, can I call you later?"

"Yeah, I have to get this homework done anyway."

"Okay, love you, Rain-drop!"

"Love you too, X!"

100. MR. TUCKER

During lunch,

Umi gets an email.

"Someone wants to be our club adviser!" Umi.

"Who?" Alyssa and I ask at the same time.

"A Mr. Tucker. Do any of you have him as a teacher?"

We both shake our heads *no*.

"He said we can meet him in the cafeteria briefly
     after school."

In the cafeteria?

Why not in his classroom?

I nod.

"Okay, cool."

After school, Alyssa, Umi, and I meet up in the cafeteria
to meet our potential club adviser.

"I wonder what subject he teaches." Umi.

"Maybe he could tutor us in something."

Alyssa laughs.

"*Right?* That'd be cool," I say.

We wait a bit as custodians clean up around us.

One of the lunch servers comes up to us.

I guess we shouldn't be in here.

Uh-oh.

"Sorry that we're here," I say. "We're waiting for a
teacher. Umi, show him the email."

"Are you guys here about the Circle Group?" he asks.

He must've seen the flyer.

Maybe he knows Mr. Tucker.

"Yeah, do you know Mr. Tucker?" Umi.

"I *am* Mr. Tucker."

"Oh," I say.

"Oh! Hi!" Alyssa.

"What are your names?" he asks with a big smile.

He sits down, pulling off his apron.

"Well, I'm Umi. That's Rain. And that's Alyssa."

He shakes all of our hands.

"Umi, Rain, and Alyssa. Beautiful names. When I

saw that flyer around, I said, we need this in this school. We've *always* needed this. I think what you guys are starting here is great. I love supporting young people in things to better themselves and their community. You all should be proud of yourselves."

We're all smiling *so, so* big.

Mr. Tucker seems like the perfect fit for Circle Group.

Mr. Tucker seems like someone who really cares.

"I'll get it signed off by Principal Bailey," he says.

"And you guys should be good to go. Like I said, we need this here."

We nod.

To be honest,

I need one of these   *everywhere*   I am.

"Thank you so much, Mr. Tucker," says Umi. "We're happy to have you on board with us."

101. JOURNAL

When I was younger, I heard that it's not good to judge a book by its cover. I think it's because covers can end up saying really little about a book. Sometimes it can give you the wrong impression. I remember one time Mommy took me to the doctor and they were giving out free books. I chose the one I thought had the prettiest cover with lots of color. I actually ended up hating the story. It was the opposite of what I was expecting. It was really boring.

I know people really say that for us not to judge people. When Mr. Tucker turned out to be one of the lunch servers, to be honest, I was a bit shocked. I thought he'd be a teacher or something.

But Mr. Tucker is so nice and so cool, and I'm glad he chose to be our adviser. So, so glad.

102. I BRING DAD UP

At my session with Dr. Sherif,   I bring Dad up.
   "So you *don't* want a relationship with your father?
      Is that what you're saying?"
she asks.

"No, I do." I clear my throat to remove the lump that
　　has expanded into a boulder.
"Do you think perhaps you could call him one
　　time and I see how it goes? Change is scary, but
　　there's good change too."
"I can try."

103. JOURNAL

Thinking about attempting to call Dad seems like
going to the dentist for a root canal. There goes
that cavity again.

104. WHILE PUTTING UP CIRCLE GROUP FLYERS

Umi's art teacher says
we can have our meetings in the art room, as long we

keep it clean
and put everything back.

Umi makes us new flyers,   this time   for *members*.

While putting up Circle Group flyers
            in a different part of the school
                    from Umi and Alyssa,
I see Tommy.

But he just walks away.

105. IN MATH CLASS

Amare turns to me and asks,
    "What time is that Circle Group club? Brenda and I
        want to go."

106. MY PHONE VIBRATES

When I get home,
my phone vibrates with a text.
I look down.   It's from Nara.
Nara?

> **Hey, Rain. What time is the Circle Group thing tomorrow?**

107. JOURNAL

I hope Circle Group goes well. I can't really sleep.
I'm so nervous. I feel anxious. I'm trying all the
breathing techniques and now I'm journaling so I
can let some of my thoughts out. Hopefully I'm
not up for too long. I know everything's going to
be okay. I pray everything's going to be okay.

108. FIRST CIRCLE GROUP MEETING

Today is the day   of our first Circle Group meeting
outside of City Middle School
                without
                        Dr. McCalla and Miss Walia,
                with
                        Me, Alyssa, Umi, and Mr. Tucker.
I tell Mom to pray an extra prayer for us.
Although I'm all nerves,   I ask Mom   a question I
        haven't asked in a long time,

                                        a question I
        forget to
        ask often.
        "Are you okay, Mommy?"
I eat a spoonful of my cereal.
She exhales,   meaning   *tired,*
but with a smile,   meaning   *trying.*
        "It's just been a lot of hours of work, but I'm okay.
                Rain, look at this."
She shows me her phone.
What's this?

It's saying something about her being a   *client.*

"What is this?" I ask.

"I signed up for some type of virtual therapy."

I remember   last year   when Xander told me she
     was   *thinking about*   therapy.
But here she is,
really going for it.   *My* mom.
                              The hero of heroes.
I jump up   excitedly.
     "No *way*, Mommy, that's so cool!"
I scroll down and see her scheduled appointments
and the therapist she's appointed to.

     "We meet this Saturday. I'm kind of nervous,"
          she says.
I can't remember the last time,   or *anytime*   Mom
     has ever said she's nervous about *anything*.
When Dad left,   she didn't say it.
When we lived in the shelter,   she didn't say it.
When bills became a mile high,   she didn't say it.
When Xander got hurt,   she didn't say it.
But now   she's free   to say it,
                              to speak her truth,
               to be her version of human,
                    to remember *her*.
I put my arm over her shoulders,
          snuggle my head into her neck.

"You'll be okay. It'll be good."
She opens her mouth to speak, closes it,
then opens it again.
"But—what do I wear?" She smiles.
We both bust out laughing.

As a cafeteria worker,
Mr. Tucker has the *connect* on snacks.
He brings   two big boxes of
leftover juice,   graham crackers,
fruit cups,   and sandwiches
    into the art room.
We have a table for the food and the sign-in sheet,
and the chairs are already formed into a circle.
All of the art stuff has been put to the side,
    protected at the art teacher's request.

We've all decided that
each week Alyssa, Umi, or I
will be the activity lead.
Umi, *of course*, was the bravest soul to volunteer
    for the first week.

I don't have the same jitters I had when I first stepped
    into Circle Group,

but it's pretty *close*.
I can't stop shaking.
My hands are   unable to hold a pen   steady.
I hope people like it here.
    "You've got this, Rain," Mr. Tucker says with a big
        smile.
I almost cry at his happiness,
    his encouragement.
I'm so glad he's here with us.

I'm also praying,   hoping, that Tommy doesn't
    show up.
I keep looking at the door,   making sure he doesn't
    walk in.
Umi leans over to me and says,
    "If he comes in here, I got you."
Of course *he* would notice.
But it makes me feel better.   *I think.*

Mr. Tucker hangs a few strings of lights and
plays soft music from his phone.
    "You all like this?" he asks.
We nod.
We *love* it.

The first people to walk in are
Amare   and Brenda,

then
Nara,
        then
Maya,   a girl who we saw at the rally,
and   then
three other people
who Mr. Tucker personally invited during lunch hours.
                I hug and shake hands with
                just about everybody.
                Nara squeezes me extra tight.

As everyone takes a seat   after getting snacks,
Mr. Tucker says,
    "Welcome, everybody. It is truly my pleasure to be
        here with you all. First things first, this is a safe
        space. Circle Group is a safe space where you'll
        be able to express yourselves freely. These three
        young people have some great activities in store
        for you all, and I hope to keep seeing you here
        each week."
He starts clapping,
then we all start clapping   and cheering.
This helps to turn my nerves   into joy.
    "Thank you, Mr. Tucker," says Umi. "So before we
        get started with names, I want to pass this roll
        of tissue of around. I just want everybody to
        take as much as they *think* they need. This is

part of an activity."
As the tissue goes around,   some take a little,
        some take a little more.
"Oh no, I'm going to be *prepared*!" Nara says.
She rolls off so much tissue   that
she makes her own little roll.
We all laugh.
    "So we're going to go around the circle and say our
        names," says Umi. "*But* you're also going to say a
        fact or more about yourself, depending on how
        many sheets of *tissue* you have. One sheet equals
        one fact."
We all turn to look at Nara.
We explode in laughter.
    "Wait, *what*?" Nara says.
            We   are   cracking up.
    "Oh no, no, no!" Nara laughs. "I thought we were
        making mummies!"
            We   are   rolling.
Umi starts us off.
    "Okay, so I'm Umi, and one fact about me is that I
        love art."
    "My name is Alyssa, and my favorite color is yellow,
        I love to cook, and my least favorite subject is
        history."
    "Hi, everyone, I'm Brenda." She pauses. "I'm the
        youngest of five, my favorite food is pizza, I like

to watch movies, and, uhh, I can't swim."

"Okay, so my name is Amare. I'm in ninth grade and I enjoy listening to music."

It's my turn.

I play with the six sheets in my hand.

What should I say?

"Hi, I'm Rain. I'm the youngest in my family also. My favorite color is blue. I love to dance. I enjoy writing. I don't like scary movies. My favorite ice cream is vanilla with rainbow sprinkles."

"Hi, everyone, I'm Maya. I'm fifteen, I run track, I'm a bit of a sneakerhead, and I love my cell phone."

We laugh.

"Hey, my name is Tahj. I like video games and have been thinking about getting into streaming."

"What's good, I'm Gordon, I'm sixteen, I eat way too much junk food, I'm the oldest, I like to travel with my family."

"My name is Isabella, but I prefer Issy. I love music. I love chilling with my friends, I guess. I really don't like liars."

"Hello again, everyone. Like I mentioned, I'm Mr. Tucker. I've worked in numerous positions in this district for over twenty years. I'm a husband and a father, and I like football and my kids, most days."

We laugh.

Nara's last to go.

"I'm Nara, and . . ." She looks over at Umi.

"It's okay, you can just do a few!" Umi.

We laugh.

"Okay, well, I'm Nara, and I'm in ninth. I like
    shopping, food, and anything involving self-
    care."

"Okay, everybody, clap it up, clap it up," Umi says.

We all clap for each other,   clap   for us just being *us*.

And with each clap,

        I can already feel it:

           that

                Circle Group is going to be
                great.

109. JOURNAL

CIRCLE GROUP WAS AMAZING!!!! I CAN'T
BELIEVE WE DID IT, WE ACTUALLY DID IT!!!!

110. WORTH FIGHTING FOR

Dr. Sherif says the bridge to healthy relationships with
    others
is a healthy relationship with ourselves.
I tell her that sometimes   at night
                         or in the morning when
                         I'm getting dressed
                         or when I'm around
                         certain groups of people
some of those old thoughts creep in   again.
Thoughts like

          you're not good enough, Rain
          you're not beautiful, Rain
          you can't do what they do, Rain.

Dr. Sherif says,
    "Self-love is not just a battle, Rain, but a war.
        Sometimes a terrible war. When one thing
        seems okay for a moment, then something else
        hits."
She pauses,
her eyes staring into my eyes,

into my soul. Then she says,
"But self-love is *always* worth fighting for. Never
forget that."

111. CIRCLE GROUP

Today in Circle Group
Alyssa asks us to share   one thing that we *want*
         and
              one thing that we *need*.
  "Well, for me . . ." Alyssa. "This is a bit personal, but
    my uncle Ricky was recently detained for his
    immigration status. I *want* him to come home.
    And I *need* my family to be complete again."
We all nod.
  "Thank you for sharing, Alyssa. Anyone can go." Mr.
    Tucker.
  "Okay, I'll go," says Sincere, who is new today. "I
    want to do good in school. And I need the
    support from my teachers and my family. Does
    that make sense?"
We all nod.

"Thank you, Sincere." Mr. Tucker. "Anyone else?"
Except his *anyone else* is really just me.
I waited to go last   because it was taking me
    forever   and a day   to think of what to say.
To think of what I want,
                              of what I need.
I clear my throat.
    "I—uhh, want to always be myself. And I need to be
        okay with being myself."
Everyone agrees;   everyone *feels me* on that one.

112. JOURNAL

Dr. Sherif says that learning about me will be
a lifelong thing. She says that I don't have to
put a lot of pressure on myself to understand
everything about me right now. She says that
she's even still learning about her. This makes me
think about X, Mommy, Dad, everybody, really.
That we all have that in common.

113. LIFTING WEIGHTS

It's been a *minute* since I've called Xander.
We've come a long way since he first got to school.
Now we talk more,   and if we don't,   *we don't*,
                                                   but then we *do*.
And that's okay.

This week
Xander texts,
My absence does not mean abandonment.
He texts,
**Remember that I forget a lot of things. Including what
    my professors said this morning!!**
He texts,
Look at Ma going to therapy like us!

When I get home from school,   I sit on the sofa and
    FaceTime him.
His background is different   yet familiar.
I hear music
    that's loud

and see lots of mirrors.

"Are you at the *gym*?" I ask.

"Yes, ma'am."

"Okay, *brolic*, big *ox*."

"You already *know*. It's been a pretty good stress
    reliever lately."

I nod, although   he's not really looking at me;
    instead he's lifting weights.

His voice   too   making me feel *lifted*,

                                    a stress reliever.

"Oh yeah, I never asked you about that girl that I
    sometimes see in your background."

"Oh yeah, good, it's none of your business anyway!"

I laugh.

"Come on, X! Is that your girlfriend or something?"

"Yup, she's a girl and my friend."

I shake my head, smiling.

"You're ridiculous."

"No, *you're* ridiculous."

I laugh,

        the weight   *lifted*   still.

114. CIRCLE GROUP

"I'm not Miss Hype Girl twenty-four seven,
    although people expect me to be," says Nara.
Today's activity,   which Mr. Tucker helped me to
    come up with,
is to speak on the   stereotypes,   labels, ideas
    that people may have about us   that may or   *may*
    not be true.
I allowed the responses to be optional because I know
how it feels
to not to know how to feel about something.
Today we also got two more people. Chance and Mekhi.
    "I'm bigger, taller. I guess I'm viewed as a threat. But
        I'm actually really quiet and really chill," says
        Mehki.
    "Why do you think people make these labels?"
        Mr. Tucker asks us.
    "I guess people do it to make themselves feel more
        comfortable," Maya says.
    "It's definitely easier to assume rather than find

out." Umi.

"I come from an army family," Tahj says. "I mean,
all of my brothers are there. So a big idea in my
family is that I'm next to go. But to be honest,
I'm not really feeling it. I'm not sure if that
decision has helped or hurt the people in my
family. Not sure if I want to take that same
path."

I think of Xander,   who shocked everybody
when he rejected his sports scholarships.
When he stopped playing   *entirely.*

"People think I'm funny, but I really just be clownin'
to keep people at a distance," Issy says.

"Same!" Gordon says.

"Definitely me!" Brenda says.

"In a way, I'm the opposite of Mehki," Amare says.

"People think I'm quiet and don't do much. But
I'm actually really into the arts."

I look at him; he looks up at me.

"What kind of arts?" Mr. Tucker.

"I . . ." He pauses. "I dance."

"You *dance?*" Nara.

"I do. Ask Rain."

I nod.

"Yeah, he does. And he's *good*," I say.

"That's what's up," Chance says.

"Facts," Gordon says.

Amare smiles, and I'm so happy   to see him free like
this.

115. JOURNAL

I think I'm going to do it. I think I'm going to
call him.

116. I CALL DAD

When I get home from school,
I sit on Xander's bed,   staring down at my phone.
Should I call him now?
I go to *Dad* in my contacts.

     I wait
    and wait.

Maybe this is a bad idea.
What will I say?
I get up,   walk around,
     sit down,
                    lie down on X's bed,
sit back up.
Breathe, Rain, breathe.
I exhale.
I can't do this.
I lock my phone,
        I unlock it.
I go back to his name.
I press the call button,   then hang up real
    quick.
Relax, Rain, relax.
I press the call button   again.
I put the phone to my ear   and   close my eyes.
    "Hello?"
His voice.
I forgot what it sounded like.
I remember what it sounds like.
                         A mix of familiar and
                              foreign.

I breathe.
    "Dad?"
    "*Ray Ray?* Is it really you?"
Immediately,   tears fall down my face.

Ray Ray.

"Yup."

"I've been calling for you."

I exhale.

"I know."

"Are you okay?"

I wipe my face with the back of my hand.

"I'm okay."

"How's school?"

"School's good."

"I'm so happy to hear from you."

I can hear it.

The smile in his voice.

Genuinely happy.　　*I think.*

　　　　　　　　　　I hope.

　　　　　　　　　　　　　　　　Dad.

117. JOURNAL

I thought I would hate talking to Dad, but I didn't. It wasn't as bad as I thought it would be. It was actually okay. It was actually kind of nice. I think I can do it again. Dr. Sherif says all relationships have to start from somewhere.

118. CIRCLE GROUP

Today at Circle Group   we have new members,
    Kasyn, Ava, and Khalil.

Umi is leading a discussion.
He asks,
    "What is something that is *unacceptable* to you in a
    relationship? Any relationship."

He holds up a small stuffed bear that we're using as our
talking piece.

Maya raises her hand;   he throws it across the
circle to her.

"Liars, *period*!"

"Period!" everyone says.

I think I have one.

I raise my hand.

Maya throws it to me.

"Inconsistency," I say.

Chance raises his hand.

I throw it to him.

"Gaslighting, one hundred percent!"

What's that?

"What's *gaslighting*?" Tahj says.

"When people act like how you feel doesn't matter,"
Alyssa says.

"Like how?" Ava says.

"Like saying you're *dragging it*," Chance says.

"Or that you're being too *dramatic*," Issy chimes in.

"Or they try to tell you that something didn't
happen the way it happened," says Mr. Tucker.

"Yeah, that's *crazy*," Gordon agrees.

Kasyn raises his hand.

Chance throws the stuffed bear to him.

"Well." Kasyn. "What I really can't deal with is
fakeness."

"That's a fact; everybody's fake now," Nara says.

"How is *everybody* fake?" asks Mr. Tucker.

"Social media!" Mehki answers.

"Big facts, social media got everybody pretending to
　　be something they're really not," says Kasyn.

We all agree.

"Everybody thinks they're a celebrity now, for real,"
　　Umi says.

"And they pretend to be happy," Khalil adds.

"And they pretend to have money." Gordon.

"Why do you think we do that, though?" asks Mr.
　　Tucker.

"For likes!" says Sincere.

"Maybe for acceptance," Umi adds.

That's true.

Kasyn lifts the bear into the air.

"Anyone else?" he asks.

Nara lifts her hand.

He throws it to her.

"Okay, hear me out," Nara says. "For me, it's
　　unacceptable if the person I'm dating has a best
　　friend that they're *too close with*!"

So many hands shoot up,　　and
everyone is laughing so hard,　　　even Mr. Tucker.

After Circle Group
when everyone's packing up to go,

Umi comes up to me.

"This is for you," he says.

He takes out something from his book bag.

It's a painting, the painting of *me*.

I take it from him and look at it,   *really* look at it.

Unlike the horror I felt last time,

this time I'm in awe.

It's actually beautiful.

An array of colors dancing in the background,

my face   with the widest smile.

"Wow, Umi, you're good."

"Thanks, it's yours. I had no intention of painting

anyone else, by the way."

I look up at him,   his eyes soft

and kind.

Oh.

"Oh."

"Rain, you know I care about you a lot."

Oh.

"Umi . . ."

He lifts his hands.

"This is not me. Dr. Sherif told me to start being

more honest."

We both laugh.

"Same." I pause. "I appreciate you a lot. You're one

of my best friends. It's better this way—being

friends."

He nods.

"I agree."

119. WHEN I GET HOME

I open the front door to see
           Mom asleep on the sofa.
I try to tiptoe my way past her.
I know she's tired from work.
I know she's tired from standing.
I know she's tired from mothering.
I know she's tired from *human-ing*.
                  She's still in her work clothes.
                  Even her shoes are still on.
  "Rain?"
I'm not as quiet as I thought.
  "Hi, Mommy, sorry to wake you."
She motions her arms for me to come over to her.
She sits up on the sofa.
I sit next to her.
  She puts
           her arm   over my shoulder.

"How was school?" she asks,
　　　her head leaned against mine,
her eyes still closed.

　　"It was pretty good. Circle Group was good."
I feel her nodding.

　　"And Alyssa? Umi?"

　　"They're good too." I pause. "How has the virtual
　　　therapy been?"
She chuckles.

　　"It's way better than I thought. For some reason, I
　　　was afraid. Maybe more intimidated. But I look
　　　forward to it now. It's a good change."
I nod.

And we just sit there,　　　quiet,

　　　　　　　　　　　quiet and okay.

120. AT CHURCH

Sade is standing at the pulpit   to introduce a
   performance.
There's applause,   and the performer
         who walks up
with their flag
                 is Amare.

Amare?
He stands there with his favorite flag, the red one,
              the one that he says
              reminds him of fire.
Once the music starts, so does Amare.
He moves with the music in such a way
      that reminds me that dance is *art*.
Gentle yet powerful.
   Like ballet mixed with martial arts.
The flag becomes fire   in his hands,
the song saying,
   I am accepted.
He spins,
he turns,

he waves,
    slow,   then fast.
People stand,
        people clap before it's over,
            people praise God because
            of what Amare can do.
People *feel*.
And tears   fall from my eyes   because he's
remembering,

        Amare is remembering himself.

121. UNCLE RICKY

I wake up to a missed call from Alyssa.
My heart sinks.
I hope nothing bad happened.
I try to call back,   but no answer.
Oh no, no, no.
I call Umi.
    "Hey, Rain."
    "Hey, Alyssa called me, and when I called back, she

didn't answer."

"Oh, really? Wait, she's calling both of us through
FaceTime right now. Let's answer."

The camera is on someone,   a guy,   but it's kind of
blurry.

The person waves.

"Hello, you two!"

I know that voice;   the image gets clearer.

Uncle Ricky?

"*Uncle Ricky?!*"

"No way! *What?!*" Umi.

I run into the living room,   where Mommy is sitting,
and start jumping up
              and down
and screaming,

"He's home! He's home! Uncle Ricky is home!"

122. TEXT FROM X

In math class, I get a text from X.
Are you remembering you today?

                                    Yeah, are you?

Have to.

123. CIRCLE GROUP

Alyssa tells us to bring magazines,   old or new,
with us to Circle Group.
Mr. Tucker gets the teachers to donate   so many
        magazines
            scattered   on the art room   tables.
The art teacher donates   poster boards
                and lends us glue sticks and scissors.

"Today," Alyssa says, "we're creating vision boards."
She tells us to find and paste images together

that represent what

we want

our futures to look like.

I never thought about my future   too deeply.

Sometimes,   *to be honest*,   it's hard to
think too far ahead.

Sometimes,   *to be honest*,   all I can
worry about is the day I'm living in.

Sometimes,   *to be honest*,   the future
seems scary.

But this,

this

is fun.

"What are you cutting out?" Umi comes over to the
table I'm at with

Kasyn, Maya, Mehki, and Chance.

"A plant?" he asks.

He chuckles.

"You want to be a gardener? Or maybe a farmer?"

I look up at him.

"Nah. But I do want to grow."

"Word." Chance daps me up.

124. JOURNAL

Progress, not perfection.

125. WE REMEMBER

Umi and Alyssa are over,
and we can't stop talking about
> how Uncle Ricky's finally home,
> how dope Circle Group is,
> how nice Dr. Sherif is,
> how ninth grade isn't all that bad.

I go into Xander's room and get his speaker.
I bring it into the living room and play it like how he

used to play it.

I play some old-school   Sam Cooke–sounding music.
                                    Then I switch it to Afrobeat,
                                                    hip-hop,
                                                        salsa,
                                                        jazz,
                         just about anything to keep us *moving*.

I bring my flag out.
I wave it around.
I let Alyssa try it,   then Umi.

                         We keep dancing.
                         We keep laughing.

The front door opens, and Mom walks in   and starts
clapping and moving her shoulders in some shimmy.
We all try to do the same.
   "Okay, Mom, I see you!" I laugh.
And although I'm hoping this moment
will never end,   I know
that we'll remember our pockets of happiness
                                    in the good,
                                        in the bad,
                                and in the change.

We will keep remembering who we are,
who I am,
myself,
me,
remembering,
always remembering
Rain.

ACKNOWLEDGMENTS

Thank You, Jesus, for healing what I couldn't on my own, for sending those who help with the process, and for the gift of passing what I've learned on to others. Thank You for progress and not perfection.

Thank you to my greatest backbone and inspiration: my family. Mommy Tetlah "ToTo" Stewart, Alisia "Lisa" Allen, Toni "TT" Comrie, Savannah "Sammy" Fisher, Julanie "JuJu" McCalla, Gordon "GG" Gaston, and Shannon "Bobby" Gordon. I love y'all. Thank you for all the support, the love, and the laughs.

To my agent-author, Rena Rossner, thank you for believing in the importance of Rain's story. I'm grateful. To my lovely editor, Alyson Day, the entire editing team, and everyone at HarperCollins who had a hand in bringing *Rain Remembers* to life—thank you for everything!

Special character-inspired shout-out to one of my mentors, Fatima Sherif: thank you for everything you do for me and others. Your brilliance and encouragement are greatly appreciated. You're the best! Also, to Mount

Vernon's own Charles Tucker, for always being such a light and inspiration to so many. Thank you!

Thank you to those who make a consistent, positive impact in my life. Your words, prayers, support, hugs, correction, jokes, and listening ears mean the world to me. Thank you; love you all.

To you, reader: keep remembering, keep rising, keep loving you, keep holding on to the truth that better is coming. You're worth it, and I believe in you. Always.

DON'T MISS THE COMPANION NOVEL!

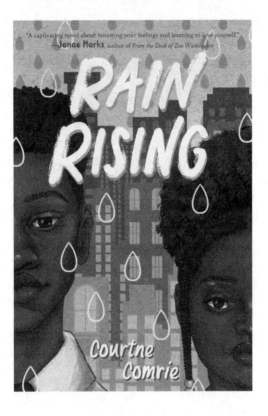